To Leave
a Shadow

Michael D. Graves

Meadowlark (an imprint of Chasing Tigers Press)
Meadowlark-books.com
Emporia, Kansas

Cover photo by Dave Leiker
daveleikerphotography.com

ISBN-13: 978-0692567791
ISBN: 0692567798

David —
Thank you for sharing your research and knowledge of Dodge City with me. I appreciate you —
Mike

To Leave a Shadow

To Leave a Shadow

Michael D. Graves

by Michael D. Graves

A 2016 Kansas Notable Book

A MEADOWLARK BOOK

Also by Michael D. Graves

Green Bike, a group novel

with Kevin Rabas and Tracy Million Simmons

Shadow of Death

All Hallows' Shadows

for my brothers
Rick and Daryl

often apart
always together

"It may be that a better way
To conquer time and the world
Is to pass, and not to leave a trace –
To pass, and not to leave a shadow
on the walls…"

Marina Tsvetaeva

Spring 1937

Black flies swarmed over the body, even before they got it out of the water. The buzzing, hissing swirl made a difficult job even harder. Two cops, one on each side of the bloated corpse, grunted and swore as they struggled against the river current. Each grabbed a hold under a limp arm and tugged against the powerful eddies, leaning backwards to gain leverage, fighting for purchase on the river bottom. The muddy water flowed over and around the soggy mass. They gasped for air and gagged when they sucked it in. The stench was thick and foul, the sort that lingers in your nostrils and wakes you late at night and puts you off your breakfast the next morning.

I smoked a cigarette and watched the struggle. It was humid, and I was perspiring. I took off my hat and wiped my brow with a handkerchief. My shirt stuck to my back. Rivulets of sweat trickled down my neck. I stuck a finger inside my collar and raised my head to take in some fresh air, but it was fruitless. To the south, a meat packing plant belched out rancid offal fumes. To the west, a bakery added a sticky, sweet cinnamon scent. The odors from the factories mingled beneath the heavy clouds and descended on the city below. It smelled like a fart in a pastry shop.

Somewhere in the distance a horn honked and then another. A church bell rang and tires rumbled over brick streets. Brakes squealed. A siren wailed in the distance and a plane flew overhead.

Several people stood around the perimeter, shifting from foot to foot, gawking and then looking away in disgust. Almost anyplace else in the city would have been more pleasant, but our species has an innate urge to observe the grotesque. Some watched, others covered their mouths or mumbled to companions, and someone bent over and gagged. Somebody swore softly, and somebody coughed.

The two policemen finally dragged the body ashore, and the buzz of the flies grew louder. The uniformed cops bent over at the waist with their hands on their knees gasping for air. I stared down at the swollen corpse and swallowed the bile rising in my throat. I thought about the poor bastard who once inhabited that body and pondered the fickleness of fate. Why him? What had he ever done? Why not him? Does anyone deserve to die like this?

I thought about his widow sitting at home, eager for him to return, and I wondered how she would react when she got the gruesome news. How else could she react? She'd crumble like a KO'd boxer. This guy wouldn't be coming home tonight or any other night. He'd never again come through the door, peck his wife on the cheek, and ask what's for dinner. She'd never again ask him about his day. His life was over, spent, wrung out of him by a muddy, roiling river. Life is fragile, life is futile, and we all cash in one way or another, but this guy had drawn a particularly lousy death. I looked down at the rotting mass and crushed my cigarette beneath my shoe. I continued to stare at the body for a long moment. I shook my head and asked myself for maybe the hundredth time why I'd ever gotten into this business.

Friday, April 16

I t began three days ago. I had just completed a case, locating a missing person, and I was beat. Some teenage kid had figured life in the big city beat living in a Kansas cow town, and who could blame her? She'd hit the road looking for fame and fortune. She figured her sweet soprano voice and long, lean gams would earn her star billing on a marquee, but she was wrong. I'd gotten to her just before hunger had driven her to sell herself on the street to put a meal in her stomach.

The case had taken me on a two week trek to Kansas City, St. Louis, and Chicago and back by railroad. I had returned the kid to grateful parents and enjoyed some good jazz in the bargain, but the travel had taken its toll. I'd slept sitting up in railcars or slumped on sagging flop house mattresses. I'd eaten peanuts and boiled eggs in saloons and burgers and beans in greasy spoons. I was exhausted and hoping to relax a bit.

I was reading the morning edition of the local rag, *The Wichita Eagle*, and getting caught up on the real world, whatever the definition of the real world is. Auto workers were at odds with management and had staged a slow-down strike in Detroit. Nothing new there. The Palace downtown was showing a film starring Don Ameche and Ann Sothern that looked pretty good. Another notice caught my eye. There was a show at the Miller starring Jean Harlow. Her photograph was at the bottom of the page, and boy did she look hot. The advertisement pictured Robert Taylor whispering into Harlow's ear. Maybe he was nibbling on it. Either way, he was holding Harlow close, and she seemed to be enjoying it. Some guys have all the luck.

I turned to the sports page. Max Baer had been soundly battered by an unknown Welshman in London, and in Baer's own words, he looked to be washed up. The Detroit Red Wings had beaten the New York Rangers and taken the Stanley Cup, but frankly, hockey doesn't thrill me. Baseball's my sport. I was interested in baseball news, but it was still a week before opening day, and the columns were mostly speculation and gossip. The White Sox had beaten the Pirates in an exhibition game in Kansas City, and prognosticators were making their usual pennant race predictions before the first pitch of the season was served up. Nothing new there, either. I tossed the paper aside and leaned back in my chair. That's when she walked in.

She opened the door and stopped at the threshold and looked around the room. I didn't know what was running through her mind, but I could imagine. Maybe she expected comfy chairs and a few begonias decorating a coffee table. Maybe she assumed a secretary would smile and greet her with, "Good day. May I help you?" If that's what she thought, she must have been disappointed. I didn't have any of that. My office was an office, nothing fancy, nothing frilly, and just the way I like it. I was its lone occupant.

The lady scanned the décor. There wasn't much to scan. I had a desk, a couple of straight-back chairs, and a rack to hang my hat on. At that particular moment, my feet were up on my desk, and my hat was on the rack. Her eyes met mine, and she spoke.

"Are you a private detective?"

"That's what it says on my license. I'm still waiting on my secret decoder ring."

"Funny."

I didn't think she meant it.

"Are you any good?"

"That depends on who you ask."

"I'm asking you."

"Then the answer is yes, but I confess to a slight prejudice."

I flashed a smile and swung my legs to the floor, motioning toward one of the straight-backed chairs. She sat down.

"My name is Pete Stone. How can I help you?"

She removed a pair of white gloves and placed them in her lap. She was a petite blonde with slate gray eyes. Her hair was cut stylishly short with ringlets coiled above her ears. I detected a mild scent of bath powder. She wore a dark blue dress with a frilly white collar and had a purse and shoes to match. She also wore a gold band and a modest sparkler on her left ring finger. She took a handkerchief out of her purse. The initials "L.H." were embroidered in gold thread on one corner. She dabbed her eyes with the handkerchief.

"My name is Lucille Hamilton. Mrs. Lucille Hamilton. My husband is Sidney J. Hamilton."

When she spoke his name, she raised her chin and drew her shoulders back a bit as if she were proud of that fact. I admired that. I offered her a cigarette, and she took it. I lit hers and one for myself and watched the smoke curl toward the ceiling.

"Go on, Mrs. Hamilton," I said. "What brings you here?"

"It's my husband. He's missing."

She dabbed at her eyes again.

"How long has he been missing?"

"Three days. He left for work Tuesday morning and didn't return that evening. I haven't seen him or heard from him since."

"Have you gone to the police?"

She looked down at her lap and nodded.

"Yes. Yes, I went right away, Tuesday evening when he didn't come home from work. I spoke to a sergeant, I believe he was,

5

and he discussed it with his superior. I think he was a lieutenant. He told me his name, but I've forgotten it. Mac something or other, I think."

McCormick.

"They said they would post a bulletin and keep an eye out for him, but there wasn't much else they could do. 'There's been no sign of foul play.' Those are the words they used. I guess they are just too busy. I don't know. I don't seem to understand much of anything right now. I only know something is wrong, and I'm afraid. I'm afraid, and I need help. So now I'm here."

Her husband had failed to come home on Tuesday. She'd gone to the police that evening, and she'd struck out. Now it was late Friday afternoon. She'd probably spent the last three days searching for a gumshoe willing to help her, and she'd reached the bottom of her list. That's where she found me. I leaned forward.

"Do you think there was foul play?" I asked.

She crushed out her cigarette in the ashtray and looked at me with wide eyes.

"Well there must be, don't you think? A man doesn't just run off for three days does he?"

I exhaled slowly and leaned back in my chair. I thought of all the men throughout the country who had done just that these past several years. Men who had lost their jobs, their families, and their pride. Men who'd been kicked in the guts by forces they could neither envision nor comprehend. Men without lives who had finally chucked it all and taken a powder, riding the rails, living in tent cities, and drifting from town to town.

"Actually, Mrs. Hamilton, they do, quite often as a matter of fact."

I paused to let that sink in.

"Tell me about you and your husband, Mrs. Hamilton."

She used the handkerchief again and began telling me her story. They had been married for five years. They had no children.

He was thirty-one years old and worked as an engineer for Stearman Aircraft. He had the job eight years ago, not long after Lloyd Stearman opened his plant here in Wichita. Mrs. Hamilton met her husband there. He was a budding young engineer on the rise, and she had been a clerk and receptionist. After they got married, she left her position to become a full-time homemaker.

Mr. and Mrs. Hamilton lived a comfortable, routine life. He left for work each day at precisely 7:30 AM and returned home each day at precisely 5:30 PM. They ate dinner at home each evening followed by the newspaper and radio shows until bedtime. On Saturday evenings they occasionally went to a picture show, and on Sunday they attended church. I idly wondered if their lovemaking was scheduled for Mondays and Thursdays, but decided not to ask.

I asked for a photograph of her husband, and she gave me one and told me it was a good likeness. It was a head shot of a man wearing gold, wire-rimmed glasses and a tie. His hair was dark, short, and neatly parted on the left side. He was smiling in the photograph, but the image suggested a serious man. I wondered if he laughed much and doubted if he did. I stared at the picture and thought about them together. I had to admit I couldn't see him running off. He had a good job with a bright future. He had an attractive wife who seemed devoted to him. It looked like he had everything going for him, but what did I know?

"You say he leaves for work every day at 7:30 in the morning. Does he drive to work?"

"Yes, we have a car. The police found it yesterday. It was parked downtown."

"Downtown? Not out at Stearman?"

The aircraft plant was on the south side of town.

"Yes, downtown, in a parking lot. The police had it towed to the station at the lot owner's request. They called me, and I picked it up at the station."

"Where is the lot located?"

She gave me the address, and I noted it in my book.

"You know it's possible your husband left the car downtown and hopped a bus or train for parts unknown."

"No, that's not possible. My husband didn't leave me."

Her gray eyes flashed, and her tiny jaw was set. I nodded.

"OK. What else can you tell me, Mrs. Hamilton? Do you have any financial problems, debts, that sort of thing?"

"No, we have no debt except the mortgage on our house. My husband takes care of our finances. He pays all the bills, but he's very careful about keeping me informed. We have a little money in the bank, not much, but some. We add a little each month. My husband and I pay cash for everything, and nothing is on credit. Our mortgage at the bank is our only debt."

We talked for a while longer, and I made some more notes in my book. No debt except their mortgage. Mr. Hamilton kept a rigid schedule. Little time for a girlfriend, and he didn't seem the type. He kept regular hours at work. That would be easy to verify, and they'd be wondering where he'd disappeared to, also. Everything was tidy, orderly, and neat. The lives of Mr. and Mrs. Hamilton held all the excitement of laundry day. At least it did until last Tuesday. Mrs. Hamilton dropped her handkerchief into her purse and snapped it shut.

"Can you help me, Mr. Stone?"

I tossed my notes onto the desk and leaned back in my chair. Sunlight shone through the window. Mrs. Hamilton appeared to be naïve, but not helpless, and she wasn't to be pitied. She was determined to find her husband. It was late Friday afternoon. She had been to the police, and they hadn't been helpful. She'd undoubtedly been to other private investigators unwilling to take her case. She'd gone to bat and struck out. The clock on my desk ticked toward 5:00. I was her last stop and her last hope. Mrs. Hamilton's eyes met mine with an open, steady gaze. She had a quiet resolve and a stubbornness that made her attractive. I liked that. It made me want to help her. It made me want to find her husband. Also, the rent was due.

"I'll snoop around, Mrs. Hamilton, ask some questions, but I don't know where it will lead. I can't promise anything."

She nodded.

"Fine, Mr. Stone. That's all I can ask."

We discussed my fee, and she wrote a check. I told her I'd stop by her home in the morning. I wanted to gather more information. I also wanted to see the Hamilton home, try to get a feel for the man. She offered a brave smile and nodded.

After she left, I glanced over my notes. They didn't look promising. Men had been running off for years now. Between the stock market crash, the Midwest drought, and the ongoing Depression, many a strong man had broken under the strain. I replayed our conversation in my mind and tried to get a fix on Hamilton. I looked at his photograph and read over my notes, but I couldn't get a clear picture of the man. I thought of that pulp fiction character, The Shadow. "Who knows what evil lurks in the hearts of men?" Indeed. Who knows?

I looked out the window at the shadows falling over the city. Men wearing suits and hats and women in dresses and high heels scurried for cars and buses. The lucky ones were headed home to warm meals and loving families, looking forward to a bit of time away from work. Some weren't so lucky. I thought about Mrs. Hamilton going home to an empty house. She was afraid and alone. I considered my own situation. I wasn't afraid, but I was alone. I didn't have a family at home. There would be no hot meal waiting for me. What I did have were a client, some notes, and a few bucks in my pocket. What I needed was a clue.

I hadn't always been a private eye. The curtain came down on the Wall Street shenanigans that black Tuesday in '29, but the final act had been choreographed for some time before that. Nearly eight years had passed since that dark day. The fat cats had feasted, and now the dinner party was over, and famine had set in. The money changers who'd never had a reason to clean grime from under their fingernails were now clawing to find work, any kind of work that would put food on the table. They no longer dined on steaks. For many, hamburger had to do – if they were lucky enough to get hamburger. Many weren't. It was the big guys who had made the rules, and it was the big guys who'd broken them trying to squeeze the last buck out of the little guy. It turned out to be a game of musical chairs, and when the music stopped playing and the scrambling began, Joe Lunch Bucket was left standing without a place to sit.

My partner and I had owned a small dairy delivery business back then. We traveled throughout the county, visiting farmers, buying up milk and eggs and butter, and delivering the products to homes in Wichita. Nothing big, but we made a living and supported two families. Times got tougher after the crash, and our little business no longer supported both households.

We thought about selling it, but we hated to let it go. Besides, who would buy it? We both knew the business would support one family, so we decided one of us would give up his share to the other. We agreed to settle it with a toss of the coin, winner take all. "All" was a panel truck, a list of suppliers, and another list of customers. When I called heads and the coin landed tails, I shook my partner's hand and wished him the best. He stood staring at his shoes, shifting his weight from one foot to the other, but I chucked him on the shoulder and told him he'd won the business fair and square. We said our goodbyes, and I never looked back.

Times worsened, and the Depression broke a lot of good folks. It also brought out the best in many people. Men worked from sunup to sundown for enough money to buy that day's groceries for their families, then went to bed at sundown and got up at sunup and did it all over again. Most people never quit. Some did. Bad times brought out the worst in some. Most folks stayed honest and did what they had to do. Others lied, cheated, and stole to get by. Some did even worse.

I decided this was where I'd cash in. There would always be a call for someone to right the wrongs and balance the scales, and I decided to become a private investigator.

I got my ticket, rented an office, and had "Pete Stone, Private Investigations" painted on the door. Business came slowly, but it came. Most of it was clean. Some of it wasn't. I've crept through the alleys in gum-soled shoes, and I've peeped into a keyhole or two, but I've made a living.

Of course, making a living isn't always enough. This type of work suits me, but I learned too late it didn't suit my wife. She resented the odd hours, the late nights, the uncertain income. The sometimes seedy clientele didn't help, either. So when our youngest joined the Navy and went east, my wife went west to live with a chinchilla rancher.

It was Friday night, and I needed a drink. I decided to go to the Green Gables, a roadhouse just outside the city limits where I could enjoy some bourbon and a hot meal. The roadhouse also offered gambling and dancing upstairs, but I just wanted a quiet meal, and I didn't want to eat on an empty stomach. I wanted booze. I hopped into my car and drove to the edge of town.

It was still early, and the place wasn't crowded yet, but people were starting to file in. The doorman and I nodded at each other with that expression of people who don't know each other by name, but recognize each other as being familiar. I made my way to the bar and took a stool. The bartender recognized me and nodded, and in a few minutes he placed a glass of Woodford Reserve bourbon over ice in front of me.

"Thanks, Sam."

"Good to see you, Pete."

We made small talk for a moment, and he moved down the bar toward other patrons. The band upstairs was playing their version of "Goody, Goody," and I tapped my foot on the bar rail while I sipped the bourbon and smoked a cigarette. Couples strolled arm in arm toward the staircase leading to the dance floor above.

The Green Gables had once been a large rambling farmhouse, but after the owners sold the farm and retired, the house had been remodeled. It was now a combination restaurant, bar, dance club, and gambling hall. Someone once told me that a few working gals entertained customers in back bedrooms, but I couldn't swear to it being true. The Gables was a great place to bring a sweetheart or spend an evening alone, but it was also a den of iniquity. It resided outside of the city limits and kept a low profile, and the local cops turned a blind eye to the goings on. Hell, on any given night, a good number of the customers might be off duty cops. Everyone at city hall knew about the club, but like an alcoholic brother-in-law, no one talked about it.

I signaled for another glass of bourbon and swiveled my stool around to look over the dining room. The clientele was mostly couples talking quietly over their meals. White shirted waiters and waitresses moved efficiently from table to table, taking orders and filling water glasses. Against the far wall at a large, round table sat maybe a dozen people, men and women. A fat man sat with his back to the wall, a blonde bimbo clutching his arm, and held court over the others. I watched him take a cigar out of his mouth and wave it before leaning over the table and speaking in a low voice. He must have said something particularly witty and charming, because the others began laughing loudly, guffawing and slapping each other on the back and doing their damndest to be the good audience. It worked, because the fat man signaled to a waiter who began pouring champagne into everyone's glass. All one big happy family.

I turned back toward the bar and sipped on my bourbon. A woman took a stool two over from mine and tapped a cigarette on a faux gold case. I leaned over and offered a light, and she thanked me. She ordered a drink with fruit and an umbrella hanging out of it, and I told Sam to put it on my tab. The lady thanked me again. I suddenly felt like company, so I moved over a stool.

"I don't believe I've seen you here before."

"I just got into town. Someone told me this was a decent place."

"It depends on your definition of decent, I guess, but the Green Gables is all right. What brings you to Wichita?"

She took a final drag on her cigarette and crushed the butt in an ashtray.

"I needed a change of scenery. I used to live in this part of the country."

I nodded.

"I like the Midwest. I've lived here all my life. Where did you come in from?"

"Denver. I got married, and my husband moved us to Denver. He's a coal miner. At least he was. Lately he's been more of a drinker. He started hitting the booze right after we got to Denver. I couldn't blame him really. Spending all day underground, coming up only after the sun went down. I don't think the poor guy saw more than a dozen sunny days in a year. Then one day he went to work drunk. He was going down the lift, and his pickax slipped out of his hand. It landed on another worker below. Luckily, it missed the guy's head, but it broke his shoulder. My husband lost his job, and he was no longer a miner. He kept on drinking, though. Not long after that he was no longer my husband. I'd had about all of Denver I needed, so I hopped on an eastbound train, and here I am."

Something caught my eye. From a far door in the corner, a young man entered the room and made his way between the tables toward the fat man. The young man, just a kid really, was dark-skinned and dressed in a blue pin-stripe suit with a white shirt and a blue tie. I recognized him immediately. He moved like a man with a purpose. The lady on the next stool looked over her shoulder.

"Somebody you know?"

"Yeah. Actually, I know his father. I helped the kid get out of some trouble once."

The young man reached the table and stood silently at the big man's elbow. When the big man acknowledged his presence, the kid slipped something out of his coat, what looked like a small paper bag, and slid it under a napkin on the table. The man shook the kid's hand, and the kid glanced at his palm and smiled. The entire transaction took just a few seconds, and the kid was gone. If I hadn't been staring right at them, I would have missed it. I whispered to myself.

"Son of a bitch."

The lady pretended not to hear. I finished my glass of bourbon and ordered a second along with another drink featuring fruit and an umbrella for the lady. It was time we introduced ourselves.

"I'm Pete Stone."

"How do you do, Pete Stone? I'm Sally Ming."

We sipped our drinks and chatted some more. The band played a Tommy Dorsey tune called "The Music Goes Round and Round." It sure does, I thought to myself. The joint was starting to jump, but I didn't feel festive, and I sensed that Sally didn't either. What we felt was loneliness.

"Are you hungry, Sally?" I asked.

She shook her head.

"Not at all," she said.

"Well, I'm not either," I said.

I tossed back the last of my bourbon and settled up at the bar while she visited the ladies room. I didn't ask her to leave with me, the arrangement was unspoken, but she took my arm when she returned from the toilet, and I led her to my car. We drove to her place, a small, tidy apartment on Murdoch Street.

She asked if I wanted anything to drink, and when I said I didn't, she came into my arms and kissed me lightly on the cheek. That led to more kissing, and soon we were undressed and doing what consenting adults do to ease the pain of loneliness. We fell onto her bed and went at each other like wild animals. I realized I had a hunger that food wouldn't satisfy, and Sally was eager, too. We laughed and lusted and giggled and groaned and spent the better part of two hours in passionate embraces before we fell back onto our pillows completely sated.

"My god, I needed that," she said.

"I feel like I've just danced the Lindy for two hours straight," I said.

Sally glanced at my manhood.

"I'll bet that never happened on the dance floor," she said.

I laughed and agreed she was right. We smoked and chatted for another hour or so, and then I kissed her goodnight. We knew we'd never see each other again, and we each knew that was okay. For one night, for a few hours, two lonely people had happened upon each other and given each other pleasure and comfort. That was enough. I kissed her one last time and drove to my place on Lewellen.

Saturday, April 17

The next morning I woke up early and showered and dressed. I scrambled a couple of eggs and washed them down with black coffee. I don't cook a lot of meals, but how can you screw up a scrambled egg? Saturday morning breakfasts used to be special. Marcie would get up early and make a big meal. Sometimes she'd whip up omelets with fresh eggs, ham, onions, and peppers. She'd usually make biscuits and sometimes gravy to pour over them. Hell, occasionally she'd even fry up a chicken. Who else eats fried chicken for breakfast? Don't knock it till you've tried it. Now she was frying chicken and making omelets for a chinchilla farmer in western Kansas. That's life.

The morning *Eagle* was on the front porch, and I brought it to the table. The headline blared over a photograph of a pair of New York crooks that had been captured in Nebraska after seriously wounding a federal agent in Topeka. On the sports page, the Yankees looked to have another dominant year, big surprise. The Yankees always had a good year. They had talented players, and they played good baseball.

I turned to the obituaries and scanned the page. There was a time when the first thing that caught my eye was the name of the deceased. Lately though, the age of the deceased is what I noticed first. I read one obituary about a forty-two year old woman whose name I recognized, Joan Longstreet. The news gave me a jolt that was followed by a surge of sadness. Joan and I had gone to high school together. I even took her to a winter dance that was aptly named the Snow Ball. I recalled how awkward and embarrassed I'd felt when I tried to pin a corsage to her gown. Her mother standing at my elbow hadn't helped, but I finally managed. Joan was a lot of laughs, and we had fun at the ball. We lost touch after high school, and I hadn't seen her for over twenty years. Now she was dead. I sipped my coffee, but it had gone cold. I didn't see the name of anyone else I recognized, but I noted that two of the others listed deceased were younger than I was. Damn.

On the editorial page, a columnist expressed concern over the expanding German Luftwaffe. Were they preparing to strike? If so, where? The world wondered. I didn't. I had other things on my mind. I tossed the paper on the table and left.

I drove to my office to make a few phone calls. My office was downtown in the Lawrence Block building at the corner of Douglas and Emporia. The building was only three stories tall, but a few of its tenants were notable citizens of Wichita. Some, including yours truly, were not. There were a couple of attorneys and oil company executives in the building. It was in the same block as the Eaton Hotel. The Eaton had a barbershop, a lunch counter, and a cigar store, all of which I frequented. It also housed a fancy club for the high rollers and the swells which I didn't frequent. No one had invited me to become a member, and I wasn't holding my breath. My office was small and tucked away on the third floor. It was sparsely furnished, as I've mentioned, but the location suited me.

Since it was Saturday, I suspected the people I wanted to see at Stearman would be away for the weekend, but I decided to call anyway. A lady answered the phone. She was pleasant, but not encouraging. I asked to speak with the vice president of engineering.

"That would be Mr. Gordon Veatch. I'm sorry, but Mr. Veatch is gone for the weekend. May I take a message?"

"Can he be reached?" I said. "It's important."

"Oh no, I'm afraid not. He's out of town."

"Where is he?"

There was a pause.

"As I said, he is out of town. He is a guest of Mr. Schaefer."

I knew from the papers that Earl Schaefer ran Stearman Aircraft.

"Yes, but where are they? Surely there's a phone where he can be reached."

Her voice lost some of its warmth.

"They are at Mr. Schaefer's cabin. They cannot be reached," she said.

"Is there a phone at the cabin? I could give them a call," I said.

"No, there is no phone at the cabin. They cannot be reached."

She was annoyed. I often annoy people. It comes with the job.

"Where is the cabin?" I asked. I've always felt that persistence pays.

"That is privileged information. I am not at liberty to say."

"Can you tell me when they'll return?"

There was a pause. She may have been counting to ten. Finally, she spoke.

"They will return on Monday morning. I'm afraid that's all the help I can give you. Good day."

I thanked her for her time, but the buzzing receiver told me I was speaking to dead air. No question about it. I was a charmer. I made a few more calls and left my office.

The parking lot Mrs. Hamilton mentioned was on Douglas a few blocks west of my office. I decided to walk. Wichita weather in April can be as fickle as a prom queen. Sometimes the sun shines, the birds sing, the flowers bloom, and you celebrate being alive. Other times the wind blows out of the southwest so hard a grown man struggles to keep his feet, or the sky turns an eerie green and black, and a deep rumble sounding like a runaway train signals a violent twister bearing down. When that happens, you run for cover like your life depends on it because it does. An April day in Kansas is a crapshoot, and you never know what you're going to get. Sometimes you get both, a beauty and a beast. On this Saturday morning, the sun was shining, the birds were singing, and I was full of hope. I stretched my legs and walked and took in the clean spring air.

The parking lot was small, tucked in between a couple of brick office buildings. The attendant was a slender man with graying temples. He had stooped shoulders and stood with his elbows tucked into his ribs as if he were trying to light a cigarette in the wind. He looked like a question mark. His khaki slacks and matching shirt were neatly pressed. On the right breast pocket of his shirt were embroidered the words "Park-a-Lot." Above the left pocket was the name, "Milton." He looked at me warily as I approached him, probably wondering why a man on foot was visiting his parking lot.

"Excuse me, may I ask you a few questions?" I said.

"You a cop?"

I get that a lot.

"Private," I said. "I'd like to talk to you about a car that was towed from here last Wednesday. Were you working on Wednesday?"

He pursed his lips.

"Yes, I was working on Wednesday. I work every day."

"Do you recall a car being towed?"

He gazed at his shoes in thought. I noticed his shoes were shined. I noticed mine weren't. He rubbed the side of his face with an open hand and stared at the ground. Was he mentally running through a list of all the cars he'd had towed last Wednesday? Or was he was trying to decide if he wanted to waste his time on a gumshoe that needed a shine? My money was on the latter. Finally, he spoke.

"Yeah, I had a car towed Wednesday. It was a Ford."

He remembered. Big surprise. I nodded and took the picture of Hamilton out of my pocket and showed him.

"Is this the owner?" I asked.

Milton took the photo and glanced at it briefly. Then he handed it back.

"Yeah, that's the guy."

"You hardly looked at that picture. Are you sure?"

"Sure, I'm sure. That's him. Look, I'm sorry I had to have the car towed, mister. But I got a business to run here, you know? I gave the guy an extra day to pick up his car, but when he didn't show on Tuesday or Wednesday, I called the cops. This lot is busy during the week. I've only got so many spaces, and I can't afford to just give one away, you know?"

"I understand, Milton, I do. I'm just surprised, that's all, that you can recall a guy so quickly with just a glance at his picture. It's been four days since he was here. You have a good memory."

Milton looked at me like I was a shortstop who'd just bobbled a routine ground ball.

"Why wouldn't I recognize him?" he said. "I've been saying good morning and good evening to him for weeks, haven't I?"

Weeks? Hamilton had been parking downtown for weeks? Why? The Stearman hangars were clear down on the south side of the city.

"What do you mean, weeks? How long exactly?"

He scratched the back of his neck.

"Look, I don't know exactly. Six or seven weeks I guess. I'm not certain."

"You keep records, don't you?" I said. "You note the plates on their tickets, right?"

"Yeah, yeah, that's right. I write that down."

"So you could check your receipts, couldn't you? Find out when he first started parking here."

Milton's face wrinkled. I was sure his plans for the morning didn't include going through several hundred parking receipts. He stared at me. I stared back. After several seconds he lowered his eyes and mumbled something before walking toward the small office in the center of the lot. I followed him.

There was only room for one in the office, so I stood outside by the door and lit a cigarette. I could hear Milton shuffling papers and grumbling to himself. I heard a few words, and they weren't ones he'd likely use in a confessional. After fifteen minutes or so he came out with a receipt in his hand.

"This is the first one," he said and handed it to me.

I noted the license plate number on the slip of paper and the date. March first. I did some calculating in my head and figured that March first had been a Monday. Almost seven weeks ago. I handed the receipt back to Milton and asked a few more questions. He didn't know much. He only saw Hamilton in the mornings and early evenings when he dropped off and picked up his car. He didn't know where he went during the day. They never discussed it.

"Thanks, Milton, you've been a big help," I said and handed him my card. "Give me a call if you think of anything else, OK?"

He stuck the card into the pocket beneath his name and said he would. I left realizing I had more questions than answers. Why would Hamilton park his car downtown every day? It seemed unusual for a guy who worked several miles south of downtown. Did he have something to hide? Why had he kept this from his wife? I felt like a dog with fleas. Every time I scratched a new itch popped up.

I walked east on Douglas toward my office and picked up my car. I drove to the corner of Main and William and stopped in front of the police station. The building had been the Central Fire Station until four years ago when the city had received New Deal money to remodel and convert the building to a police station. Now the station was modern and attractive in a new Art Deco style.

I wanted to talk to Lieutenant Thaddeus McCormick. McCormick was an Irish cop who'd started as a flatfoot on a beat nearly twenty years ago and worked his way up through the ranks. Like many cops, he had little time for private detectives, but he tolerated me. A couple of years back I was working on a case for a prominent citizen whose kid had gotten involved with drugs. During the course of the investigation, I uncovered a drug ring working in the city. I got my client's kid out of harm's way and blew the whistle on a big cocaine deal. McCormick and his men made several arrests, and *The Eagle* ran his picture above a three column story on page one. The good publicity scored points at city hall.

Mac didn't forget who gave him the tip. From time to time he'd leave a file open here or turn a deaf ear there when it made a dick's life easier. Of course, I remembered him at Christmas, too. I'd quietly leave a bottle of bourbon on his desk or palm him a couple of bucks. The thing about Christmas in this business is that it isn't always on the calendar, and it comes more than once a year. I found him hunched over his desk in his office, a cigar clenched in his teeth. The pungent odor of cheap tobacco hung in the air.

"Why don't you go to a ballgame or the fights or something, Mac?" I asked. "It's Saturday for Chrissake. And while you're at it, buy a decent cigar."

He grunted and took the stogie out of his face. Mac was a big guy, tall and rangy with knobs for knees and elbows. His thinning hair was slicked straight back, and his long face had grown a bit jowly these past few years. When he spoke, his voice filled every corner of the room, like a radio turned too loud.

"Get out of here, Stone. I'm busy."

This was his standard greeting. I ignored it.

"I need your help," I said.

He grunted again.

"Like hell you do."

I didn't say anything. I didn't budge either.

"Crime never sleeps, Stone," he said.

"Jeez, Mac, did you just make that up?"

"Don't be a smart ass. What are you up to? Dogging some poor slob who's banging strange tail?"

He laughed. I didn't.

"I'm looking for a missing person, an engineer who works out at Stearman. His name is Hamilton. His wife came by to see me yesterday."

He rubbed his chin with the back of his hand. It rasped like sandpaper.

"Yeah, I remember. Little blonde dame built like a sparrow. She was in here the other day. Her husband walked out, didn't he?"

"Well, he didn't come home. I don't know yet if he walked out. Have you heard anything?"

"Naw, nothing. We towed his car from a lot downtown, but we haven't heard anything."

"Why wouldn't he take his car?" I said.

"Who knows? Maybe he left it for the little lady. Felt guilty about running out and decided to go by bus or a train. It happens."

"Could be, but I have doubts," I said.

"Yeah, I'll bet you have doubts. I'll bet you also have a few of his wife's bucks tucked into your pocket."

I let that pass.

"Let me know if you hear anything, will you, Lieutenant?" I said.

"Yeah, yeah, our first priority is to make sure you get everything you need, Stone. We exist to make your life easier."

I said nothing, but I reached over his desk. He shook my hand and made the bill in my palm disappear.

"If anything comes up, I'll let you know," he said.

He brushed me off with the back of his hand, but his word was good. I left.

From the station, I drove to Douglas Avenue and turned west. I neared the bridge spanning the Arkansas River and noticed a number of ducks paddling and feeding on the water. They dunked below the surface, tails sticking straight up in the air, and came up squawking. I crossed over the river and drove toward the Clarence Street address Mrs. Hamilton had given me. My car rumbled over the brick street past several modest, new homes. When I reached hers, I pulled over to the curb and turned off the car. I leaned back against the seat, lit a cigarette, and looked over the quiet neighborhood.

The Hamiltons lived in a white frame home on the east side of Clarence two doors down from First Street. A couple of gnarled catalpa trees stood in front of their home. It would be another month before they sported their white blossoms. I always looked forward to the blooming catalpas in May. Across the street from the Hamiltons, a similar frame home sat behind a row of maples. A few maple seeds twirled in the wind and gathered on the brick street below. Beneath the front windows, a woman on her knees worked in a bed of tulips with a small garden spade. She looked to be in her late twenties. White peonies bloomed on each side of the front steps, and roses climbed a trellis on the porch. I got out of my roadster and crushed my cigarette in the street. I crossed over to where the woman was working in her garden. The pleasant smell of spring flowers rose up to greet me.

"Excuse me," I said. "May I ask you a few questions?"

She pushed a straw hat back with her forearm and smiled up at me.

"You look like a cop," she said.

"Private," I said. "Your neighbor is my client." I nodded toward the Hamilton home.

"Oh, yes," she said. "I spoke to Lucille yesterday. She said she was going to hire someone. Poor Lucille. I hope Mr. Hamilton is alright."

"So you know the Hamiltons? Good. Have you noticed anything unusual recently?"

Her eyes widened and her smile grew bigger. She was a brunette with dark eyebrows and eyes somewhere between brown and green. Hazel, I suppose. She had a too wide mouth with too thick lips and a large nose. She was not pretty, really, but her healthy complexion and friendly smile made her attractive.

"Unusual? Are you kidding?" she said. "The Hamiltons are the most ordinary people in the world. Nothing unusual happens to them."

"And yet Mr. Hamilton is missing," I said. "That's unusual, isn't it?"

Her face darkened and she squinted at the Hamilton home.

"Yes," she said. "That is unusual."

"You say you spoke to Mrs. Hamilton yesterday. When did you last see Mr. Hamilton?"

Her forehead creased.

"Let's see. Tuesday morning, I guess."

I nodded.

"Tuesday morning," I said. "Was that when he left for work?"

"No, no, I didn't see him leave for work. This was later, mid-morning, I suppose. I was right here in the garden when he came home."

She stood up when she said this. She looked toward the Hamilton home and squinted. I noticed a spider on her shoulder, one of those big, ugly numbers that hang around in gardens. A wolf spider, I think they're called. She must have read the expression on my face, and she looked down at her shoulder. To my surprise she didn't register alarm at all. She just smiled and placed her palm next to the spider and waited patiently for it to climb aboard. When it did, she bent over and let it loose in the garden.

"They eat a lot of insects," she said.

The spider disappeared among the tulips.

"Wow," I said, "I'm impressed."

She smiled.

"Did you speak to him?" I asked.

"Pardon me?"

"Mr. Hamilton. Did you speak to him?"

"No, no, he went right in. A while later he came back out, got into his car, and drove away."

"How long was he home?"

"Just a few minutes. Maybe ten or fifteen, I guess. I didn't really pay attention."

I made some notes in my book.

"And that was the last time you saw him?" I said.

She nodded.

"I haven't seen him since Tuesday morning."

I asked for her name, and she told me it was Alice Bennett. I wrote that down along with her phone number and address and gave her my card.

"Give me a call if you think of anything else, will you, please?" I asked.

She held my card close to her face and frowned for a moment before sighing and reaching into her apron for a pair of glasses. She put them on and studied my card.

"I'd be happy to call, Mr. Stone," she said. "I do hope Mr. Hamilton returns soon."

"Thank you, Mrs. Bennett," I said. "You've been very helpful."

"Glad to help, Mr. Stone," she said. "Lucille is such a doll and a good neighbor, too. We haven't had coffee together in too long. I wonder if her husband ran off."

I shrugged and thanked her again. I walked across the street toward the Hamilton house. A kid rode down the street on a green bike followed by another kid towing a beat up wagon. A third kid, smaller than the other two ran behind them, crying for them to slow down. I let the parade pass by and went up the walk to the porch steps. Mrs. Hamilton opened the door on the first knock. She must have been watching me through the window.

She invited me in and led me to the living room. Her home was small but neat and tastefully furnished. A sofa rested beneath the picture window with a coffee table in front of it. Next to the sofa a Detrola model radio sat on a small table. A fireplace was across the room flanked by matching wingback chairs. Lace doilies covered their arms and headrests. Mrs. Hamilton directed me to one of the chairs. I sat down just as a man entered the room. I stood again and waited for introductions.

"Mr. Stone, this is James Ireland, my husband's closest and oldest friend. He's a dear friend of mine, too. I asked him to be here this morning."

We shook hands, and I sat down again. Ireland took the other wingback chair.

"Would you like some coffee, Mr. Stone? I just made a fresh pot."

I said I would and told her I would drink it black. She left the room.

"So you and Mr. Hamilton are close friends," I said.

Ireland smiled.

"Yes, we go way back, all the way to grade school. I've never had another friend like Sidney. He's like a brother to me."

Mrs. Hamilton returned carrying a tray with china cups on saucers. She smiled when she heard Ireland's remark and set the tray on the coffee table. Two cups looked heavy on the cream. The third was black. She handed that one to me and took a seat on the sofa. The coffee was strong and delicious.

"Have you found out anything yet, Mr. Stone?" she said.

"Not much, but I've contacted the police. They'll let me know if anything turns up." I glanced at my notes. "Mrs. Hamilton, you told me that Mr. Hamilton leaves for work each day at 7:30. Is that right?"

"Yes, that's right. He's very punctual. He's never late for work."

"Does he ever come home during the day, for lunch perhaps?"

"No, he usually eats in his office. He doesn't take time to come home for lunch."

"Did your husband return home last Tuesday morning?"

"No. Like I said, he left for work that morning, and I haven't seen him since."

Ireland fidgeted a bit in his chair. He looked like he wanted to speak, but I wanted Mrs. Hamilton to finish her thought. Her face turned into a frown. A clock ticked on the mantel. Its round face was mounted on a polished mahogany base. I could see it was a Chelsea Brass Marine, a very nice clock.

"Wait a minute," she said. "I just remembered. I was gone Tuesday morning. I went to the beauty parlor. I go every Tuesday morning. I leave home at 9:45 for my regular ten o'clock appointment so I wasn't home all morning. Why? Is that important?"

"I don't know," I said. "I'm just gathering information now. If Mr. Hamilton takes your car to work, how do you get to the beauty parlor?"

"Oh, it's just a short walk, only a few blocks. It's good for me to walk."

She frowned again.

"What did Alice tell you?"

"Your neighbor said that Mr. Hamilton returned home Tuesday morning. He stayed briefly and left. Do you have any idea why he would do that?" I said.

She bit on the end of her thumb and shook her head. Ireland leaned forward but didn't speak.

"No, no. Maybe he forgot something, I guess, but it is unusual. Is this important, Mr. Stone?"

"Probably not," I said. "Like you say, he probably forgot something."

We talked some more about Mr. Hamilton, his interests and his habits, and I scribbled in my notebook. I was still trying to get a feel for the man. An image was forming in my mind, but I needed more. Mrs. Hamilton said he didn't keep a journal, but he kept a calendar on his desk here at home. She rose to get it, and I asked her if she had any other recent photos, also. She said she did and excused herself. I tucked my notebook into my coat pocket and stood up.

"Is there anything you can add to this, Mr. Ireland?"

Ireland furrowed his brow.

"No, I'm afraid there isn't. I wish I could help. I hope Sidney is okay."

"I sensed there was something you wanted to say a few moments ago."

"No. I wish I had something more to add, but Sidney certainly never said anything about leaving. I have no idea where he could have gone."

I turned toward the mantel. I wanted to admire Hamilton's clock. The polished brass timepiece was manufactured by the Chelsea Clock Company of Massachusetts. They'd been making clocks since before the turn of the century, and their work was highly regarded by clock collectors. I've long appreciated a well-made clock.

A small brass plate was mounted on the foundation just beneath the clock. I read the inscription on the plate. "Time is the justice that examines all offenders." The quote triggered something in my mind, but I couldn't determine what it was. It sounded vaguely familiar, but I couldn't place it. I noted it in my book just as Mrs. Hamilton returned.

"Sidney loves that clock," she said. "Are you a clock fancier, Mr. Stone?"

I nodded. "Yes, I am, as a matter of fact," I said. "I keep a few at home, several actually. I find them peaceful. I enjoy their steady ticking, and I enjoy listening to their tones striking on the hour. Clocks bring security and order to a sometimes chaotic world."

"Why, that's lovely, Mr. Stone, and you're right. They do, don't they?"

"Did you find a photo?" I asked.

"Yes, I did."

She handed me several photos along with Sidney's calendar. One of the photos was a head shot, and another had him posing in a suit and tie standing before the mantel here in the living room. A few more were casual shots taken outdoors, at a picnic or company function perhaps. One showed both Mr. and Mrs. Hamilton sitting on grass beneath a tree.

"These are fine, Mrs. Hamilton."

"I thought you might want to look at this, too," she said and handed me a bound book.

It was a college annual from Municipal University of Wichita, Class of 1929. We sat down, and I thumbed through the pages while we all sipped our coffee. I offered cigarettes, and Mrs. Hamilton took one, but Mr. Ireland declined.

"Sidney is mentioned several times," she said with a note of pride.

"Yes, Sidney was very well liked and appreciated in college," Ireland said.

Indeed he was. He'd been a member of the chess club, a scholastic engineering society, the German club, and an honors student. I noticed Ireland's picture in several of the club shots, too, and commented on it. Ireland smiled.

"Yes, like I said, Sidney and I do a lot of things together. If one of us joined a club, the other went along."

We spent some time looking over the material with Mrs. Hamilton and Ireland providing commentary. Mrs. Hamilton refilled our cups. After some time Ireland looked at his watch and stood up.

"I'm sorry, Lucille, but I have to leave. I have an appointment. Mr. Stone, it was a pleasure meeting you. If there's anything I can do, please let me know."

I stood up, also.

"I'm sorry you have to go, Mr. Ireland. I'd like to speak with you some more. When can I call you?"

"How about Monday morning?" He gave me his number but added, "I'm often away from the phone. How about letting me call you? Give me your card, and I'll call you Monday."

I had lots of questions and had hoped to ask them today, but what could I do? I gave him my card. He shook my hand, gave Mrs. Hamilton a brief hug and left.

I decided to leave, also. I had the materials I needed. I tucked the yearbook and calendar under my arm and put the photos in my pocket.

"These will be very helpful, Mrs. Hamilton. I'm sorry I wasn't able to visit with Mr. Ireland a bit longer, but it'll have to wait until Monday."

"Yes, he's very busy, I'm afraid."

"I didn't get to ask him what he does for a living."

Mrs. Hamilton chuckled.

"Didn't I tell you? Why, he works at Stearman, along with Sidney. He's an engineer, too. They are as inseparable today as they were as children."

I should have guessed, I suppose. Of course they worked together.

"I guess you've known Mr. Ireland as long as you've known your husband," I said.

Mrs. Hamilton smiled.

"Actually, I've known James exactly one day longer."

My puzzled expression begged for an explanation.

"You see, Mr. Stone, James asked me out on a date shortly after I went to work at Stearman. It was very casual, nothing serious, but the next day he introduced me to Sidney. The moment I met Sidney, I knew he was the one. I think he felt the same thing, too. It wasn't long before we were a couple and then husband and wife."

Mrs. Hamilton led me to the door.

"Thank you, Mr. Stone," she said, "I'm so glad you are handling this. I'm very worried, and I do appreciate your help."

I nodded. I wished I could say something reassuring, but I couldn't.

"I'll let you know when I find something," I said, and I left.

I drove around the area for a few blocks, looking without knowing what I was looking for, trying to get a feel for the neighborhood. I wanted to observe. People were doing what they do on Saturday afternoons, mowing the grass, painting shutters, sweeping the sidewalks, washing the car. Kids in a small park were playing a pickup game of baseball with a tattered ball and a cracked bat that had been nailed back together. Their chatter filled the air. Ordinary folks doing ordinary things on an ordinary weekend, blissfully unaware that one of their neighbors was missing.

After a while I realized I wasn't getting anywhere, and I glanced at my watch. It was nearly suppertime, and my stomach reminded me I'd been living on nothing but coffee and cigarettes since breakfast. I turned east on Douglas headed toward downtown. I neared the Nu-Way Café and started to pull in for a burger, when I realized I'd rather have a beer with a sandwich. I turned on Seneca and pulled up at Tom's Inn.

I love a saloon. I always have. I love the smells and the sounds, the smoke hanging in the air, the low murmur of fellow beings, the dark corners and the shadows. I feel at home. When I was a kid my dad sent me to the saloon every day just before the dinner bell rang to fetch a small pail of foamy beer. I never complained. It was my favorite chore. The scents of wood and tobacco and beer and hot peanuts draw me to a bar like a hound sniffing a fox. Tom's Inn brought back those childhood memories every time I came through the door.

Tom was behind the bar working the stick when I came in. He tilted an icy mug under the tap and drew off a beer that foamed over the top.

"Draw one for me, will you, Tom?" I said.

"Coming right up, Pete," he said without looking up.

Tom's tavern featured a mahogany bar surrounded by a dark wood interior. Tom kept Storz beer on tap, and he poured a lot of it.

"And if Mabel is in the kitchen, put a pastrami on rye right next to it," I said.

"On the way, Pete," said a feminine voice through the doorway next to the bar.

I sat down on a stool, and the beer arrived as I got settled. I took a long swallow and let my eyes adjust to the dim lighting. I recognized a regular customer at the other end of the bar, but we'd never met. He was a big guy with sleeves rolled above the elbow over muscular forearms. He had a heavy jaw and a prominent nose beneath deep set eyes. His face belonged on the front of a buffalo nickel.

He often was sitting at the bar when I stopped in. I was sure I'd heard his name before, but I couldn't remember it. He wore his usual bib overalls with a greasy rag in the back pocket. I took him for an auto mechanic, probably with a shop in the area. He nodded hello, and I nodded back.

Three men wearing rumpled suits sat at a table in the center of the tavern and provided much of the background noise. Blue smoke from their cigars hung over their table. Their loud voices suggested they'd had more than a few beers each. From their conversation I gathered they were insurance salesmen, laughing and congratulating each other with stories about their weekly victories. Their collars were open, and they'd loosened the knots in their ties.

Along the wall, a young couple shared a booth, sipping beer quietly, talking and smiling, and occasionally touching hands across the table. Maybe they were in love or maybe they were just lonely and needed one another. Maybe they were agreeing to share a Saturday evening together. Maybe the Saturday evening would ease into Sunday morning breakfast. At least that's what it looked like to me. How the hell would I know? I was just playing detective.

"Here ya go, Pete."

Mabel set a hot sandwich next to my elbow.

"Thanks, Mabel," I said with a nod. The sandwich featured a generous helping of shaved pastrami on thick rye bread sliced diagonally into halves. Between them rested a dill pickle. Mabel had also added a dollop of the spicy mustard she knew I liked. She waited while I spread mustard onto the sandwich and took a bite. I hadn't realized how hungry I was. I uttered an appreciative "umm," and she smiled her approval.

"Delicious as always, Mabel. Thanks, sweetheart."

Mabel smiled again and patted my wrist before toddling back to the kitchen.

"So what's up, Pete?" Tom said. "Anything shaking?"

I swallowed and nodded.

"Yeah, I'm working on a case. Missing person."

I wiped my hands on a napkin and reached into my breast pocket. I took out the photograph of Hamilton and handed it to Tom.

"Ever see this guy?"

He studied the picture for a moment and shook his head. He took the picture to the guy at the other end of the bar.

"Larry, have you ever seen this guy?" Tom said.

Larry. That was the guy's name, Larry the mechanic. He looked at the picture and shook his head.

"No, I've never seen him," he said. "I don't know him."

Tom returned the picture. I nodded my thanks and ordered another beer for me and one for Larry. Larry hoisted his toward me and took a sip.

I finished my sandwich and started to slip the picture back into my pocket, but then I had a hunch. I looked over at the table of insurance salesmen. Maybe if a guy goes missing, I reasoned, he might buy some insurance first. Sometimes in this business, all you have to work with is a hunch. I decided to play this one.

Their conversation had taken a turn. They'd finished their discussion of the previous week's high jinks and had started talking about strange, small animals they had dined on over the years. Each one told a story, trying to one-up the others.

"My daddy, he used to deep fry muskrat every Christmas. Stunk up the whole house and pissed Momma off, every year. God, it was awful."

"Hey, my daddy taught me how to barbeque a coon. Tastes good, too!"

"I've had barbequed raccoon. It's good."

"You boys ever had possum?"

"Yeah, we used to eat possum a lot."

"I know a guy who ate an armadillo."

"Oh yeah? How'd he eat it? On the half-shell? Haw, haw."

Laughter and pounding on the table. I was glad I had finished my sandwich.

"Excuse me, gentlemen," I said. "May I interrupt for a moment?"

Their laughter died, and they looked up at me through bleary eyes. They sat up as straight as they could, like school boys caught in a prank. They took me for a cop, and I didn't discourage the idea. They probably thought they'd done something wrong, but I told them about my search for a missing person and held up the picture of Hamilton. That changed their attitudes, and they suddenly became a trio of fat ladies at the opera all wanting to sing the aria.

"Say, lemme see that."

"This guy looks kinda familiar."

"Didn't he use to hang out at Kelly's bar over on Emporia?"

"Naw, that guy didn't wear peepers, and he didn't have this much hair."

"Is this the desk clerk at the Allis? I stayed there a coupla months ago."

They passed the photograph around, and each man studied it and commented, but it was clear they didn't know Hamilton. They were just three guys who'd had too much to drink trying to be helpful. They seemed a bit disappointed they had nothing to offer. I thanked them anyway. I decided not to buy them a round of beer. They'd had enough. I also decided not to show the picture to the couple in the booth. I'd already used up my hunch for the day, and it hadn't panned out. Did I mention that most of my hunches don't?

I went back to the bar and sat down on the stool. I had another cold beer and then another one after that, and pretty soon Tom and I were talking about old friends, taverns we'd visited, and would the Yankees win it all again this season. The afternoon slid into the evening, and for a few pleasant hours I pretended I wasn't a gumshoe.

When I decided I'd had enough, I bade goodnight to Tom and Mabel. The insurance salesmen were still sitting around their table swigging beer and telling lies, and Larry the mechanic was still at the bar, but the young couple had moved on, and a lively neighborhood crowd had taken their place.

I walked to my car parked at the curb and noticed it seemed to be leaning to one side. At first I blamed the tilt on too much beer and figured my perception was altered. But as I drew near and stepped off the curb, I discovered the problem. Both tires on the driver's side had been slashed with a knife.

"Damn it," I muttered to the empty street and cursed the idle vandals that had done this. Then I noticed something on the front seat beneath the steering wheel. I opened the door, and a newspaper lay open. On top of the newspaper was a rock that had once been fist sized, but now it lay crushed into a number of smaller pieces. It wasn't exactly the mafia message of a dead fish meaning he sleeps with the fishes. Still, the symbolism was clear… crushed stone. Somebody was trying to get my attention.

Sunday, April 18

The beer and smoke put me into a deep sleep, but I woke up too early the next morning feeling fuzzy in the head. I turned on the radio and heard Uncle Ben Hammond reading the funnies. That meant it was Sunday. I listened to him narrate the weekly antics of cartoon characters while I got dressed. Blondie and Dagwood were in the middle of one of their running gags involving another impossibly tall sandwich. Annie and Daddy Warbucks took a few jabs at FDR. Daisy Mae continued her quest to snare the dense Li'l Abner, and Dick Tracy capitalized on wits and gadgetry to close in on another villain. Lucky Dick Tracy. I pondered my own lack of wits and gadgets and got dressed. I had a beer hangover, and I hadn't had enough sleep. I wasn't looking forward to another day of detecting, but it's what I do, so I finished getting ready and left.

I drove over to the Broadview Hotel for my Sunday ritual of breakfast, newspaper, cigar, and shoeshine. The night before, Larry the mechanic had supplied a couple of used tires, and fortunately there was no other damage to my car.

The Broadview was a classy hotel on Douglas just east of the river. It was a bit ritzy for my style, but I treated myself to its ambience once a week. Hanging chandeliers glistened from high ceilings. Deep carpet and flocked wallpaper suggested subdued elegance while damping the noise in the busy lobby.

The first thing I did when I was seated in the dining room was order a cup of strong, black coffee. It brought me back to life. I also ordered a huge country breakfast just like Grandma used to make. There's nothing better than a plate of scrambled eggs, country bacon, and biscuits and gravy to make a man feel like all is well with the world, at least his little corner of it. The waitress set the platter on the table and stood over me as I started eating. She smiled and refilled my coffee cup.

"Thank you, Agnes," I said.

"You have a good appetite, Pete," she said. "I like a man with gusto."

The way she said "gusto" made it sound like she wasn't referring to just the food. She winked at me. I returned her smile and watched her as she moved to another table.

Agnes had once told me her plans for leaving Wichita and settling in a bigger town, Kansas City or maybe even Chicago. She had a voice and a great pair of legs, and she thought she might make it as a night club singer or a hoofer on the stage. She talked about it for years, but she never got around to making it happen. Over time her school girl dreams faded. Her once slender hips had widened a bit, and her face had grown fuller, but she still had those great legs. She occasionally spoke of her dreams, but now her voice had a wistful tone.

I sopped up the last bit of gravy with a biscuit and washed it down with coffee. Agnes came by again to refill my cup.

"How about dinner and drinks, Agnes?" I said, "soon."

"Anytime, Pete, anytime."

She gave me another smile and disappeared into the kitchen. I sipped my coffee and mulled over that bit about Hamilton returning home from work on Tuesday morning. Why had he returned home? Had he forgotten something? It seemed out of character. It wasn't much, but the guy was so organized and attentive to detail I couldn't imagine him being forgetful. I also thought about my slit tires and the pile of stones in my car. What the hell was that about?

I paid my bill and strolled into the lobby. I bought a paper and cigar and took a seat in an overstuffed chair. A uniformed bellhop chatted with the concierge. An old, gray custodian shuffled through the lobby emptying ashtrays. Well-dressed men and women were scattered about the lobby reading newspapers or talking quietly.

After I finished my cigar, I noticed my scuffed shoes and moved toward the shoeshine stand. It stood along the east wall of the lobby. The shine boy had a customer, so I took the next chair. The customer introduced himself to me as a hardware salesman from Des Moines, in town for a convention. He held forth with great enthusiasm about the latest developments in potato peelers and vegetable dicers. I pretended to be interested, and the shine boy popped his rag and offered up a "yassuh" or a "no suh" at appropriate intervals, keeping his eyes on his work.

I opened my copy of *The Wichita Eagle* and scanned the news. Dust storms continued to ravage the Midwest. Wind-weary families, once driven by dreams of owning and farming their own little slices of America, were pulling up stakes and limping west toward new dreams of low hanging fruit and easy riches in sunny California. War clouds were forming in Asia, the same thing in Europe. *The Eagle* was a barrel of laughs. I tossed it onto a table.

The salesman paid for his shine, offered a nickel tip with a flourish, and ambled toward the elevators. The shine boy moved over to my chair and placed his box at his side.

"Yassuh," he said, staring at my shoes.

A couple of guys in dark suits walked by, murmuring in low voices. I couldn't make out what they were saying, but they were distinctly foreign, German possibly.

"Can the 'yassuhs,' Waldo," I said. "It's me."

Waldo looked up and smiled.

"Good morning, Mr. Stone," he said, "nice to see you."

"Nice to see you, too," I said. "What's new?"

Waldo stuck three fingers into a can of black polish and smeared it onto my oxfords, rubbing it evenly over both shoes, working it into the creases and cracks of the leather. His hands moved rapidly and efficiently.

"Nothing new, Mr. Stone," he said. "I just keep on keeping on."

He finished applying the polish and started buffing it with his rag. I marveled at the speed of the rag and its crisp "pops."

"Is business okay?"

"Yeah, business is fine. I don't do too bad on tips, that last gentlemen being an exception. The hotel still caters to businessmen who appreciate a good shine. I can't complain. Wouldn't do me any good if I did."

"That's good, Waldo. And the missus?"

"Oh, she's fine, too. Sassy as ever, she is. Her momma took sick and has come to stay with us for a while, but she's feeling better, and those two women sure do enjoy each other's company. Her momma is good with the little ones, too, and that helps out a lot."

"How about Ralph, Waldo? How's he doing?"

The rag paused in the air for just a moment then went back to jumping and popping. Waldo was silent for a moment and then spoke.

"Oh, not too bad, I guess. Nothing to bother you about."

"What's up, Waldo? Don't worry about bothering me. Is he involved in drugs?"

Waldo continued shining my shoes. Waldo's first name was Ellis, but in all the years I'd known him, he'd always gone by his last name, Waldo. I had tried to get him to call me Pete, but he always refused. He just couldn't bring himself to call a white man by his first name. I would always be Mr. Stone to him. Some time back, Ellis Waldo's oldest son, Ralph, had gotten mixed up with a bad element. Some jazz musicians on the south side had introduced him to marijuana. They'd lured him into carrying their drugs in exchange for free joints. An undercover cop busted Ralph with the drugs, and he'd ended up downtown behind bars.

I'd spoken to Thad McCormick to see what he could do, and he in turn spoke to the prosecuting attorney. Ralph had broken the law, but he was just a teenager, and the prosecutor could see he was a victim. He wanted the real villains, the dealers. Ralph offered up some information, and in exchange the prosecutor let Ralph walk. I really hadn't done much, but Waldo never let me forget what I'd done to help his son. The rag kept flying and popping.

"What's the trouble, Waldo?" I asked.

The veins on his neck bulged.

"Ralph is too damn stubborn and independent. He's such a bright kid, but I worry about him, Mr. Stone. I surely do."

"What's going on?"

"I don't know for sure. I have my suspicions, but I truly don't know."

"What are your suspicions?"

Waldo held his rag in midair and looked up at me.

"He's hanging around the south side again, out until all hours of the night. Sleeps late, leaves in the evening, and stays out all night again. I don't know what he's doing, but like I say, I've got my suspicions."

I did, too, but I didn't tell Waldo I'd seen Ralph at the Green Gables Friday night. I let him continue.

"I've begged him to go to school, but he doesn't see the need. He always seems to have enough jingle in his jeans to get by as it is. He's smart enough to go to college, you know. He could get a good job, maybe even be a teacher. He's smart as a whip, and he can write, too. You should read some of the stories he's written,

Mr. Stone. Good stuff, stuff that could get published. But he just shrugs it off and says there's no future for a black writer in this country. I'm plenty worried."

"Where does he hang out?"

"Oh, there are lots of places. He follows the action. Depends on who's in town and where they're playing. Lately, I think he's been hanging around the Kaliko Kat on South Broadway."

"Maybe I'll stop in at the Kaliko for a drink one night. I like jazz as much as the next guy. Don't worry, Waldo," I said. "I have a feeling everything will work out."

"I don't want to cause you any worry, Mr. Stone."

Waldo was finishing up, and I told him again not to worry. I started to pay him and suddenly remembered something.

"Say Waldo, I read something yesterday and wonder if you could place it. It's a quote that sounds vaguely familiar. 'Time is the justice that examines all offenders.' Does that ring a bell?"

Waldo pursed his lips and lowered his eyes in thought. He scratched his cheek for a few seconds and then looked up and smiled.

"It sure does, Mr. Stone. It sounds familiar. That's Mr. William Shakespeare. It comes from his play, *As You Like It.* I don't think the quote is exact, though, but I'm sure that's where it's from."

Amazing. Over the years I must've asked Waldo dozens of questions about all sorts of literature, novels, poetry, short stories, you name it, and I'd never stumped the man. He hadn't acquired his knowledge in school. He was self-educated, and he was the most well-read man I'd ever met. I like to read, and I do as often as time allows, but I wasn't anywhere near the league this man was in. He was simply one of the most brilliant people I'd ever known. In spite of that brilliance, society had given him a place. Society deemed him fit to shine shoes.

"Thanks, Waldo, you're the best."

I admired my shined shoes and wished Milton from the parking lot were here to see them, too. I paid Waldo for the shine and gave him a tip. It was more than a nickel.

Monday, April 19
Monday, April 19

T
he phone call came Monday morning, but it wasn't the phone call from James Ireland that I had been expecting. This call was from Lieutenant Thaddeus McCormick, and it was the one I had been dreading.

Generally I love mornings when the day is just beginning and still holds promise and hope. This Monday morning was special. This Monday was Opening Day for major league baseball, the day every red-blooded American male waited for all winter, the real beginning of spring. On this day a tall, lanky kid from no-where-ville would straddle the mound, rub a little saliva into the horsehide, and fire the first pitch, signaling the end of the dark season, that time with no baseball. I had looked forward to Opening Day every year for as long as I could remember.

The Phillies were scheduled to play a doubleheader against the Boston Bees, and the Athletics were opening against the Senators in Washington. Those places were a million miles away, and none of that mattered after the phone rang.

"Stone, this is McCormick. We've found a floater in the river. I've sent some uniforms over to seal off the area."

McCormick gave me the location and told me to meet him there. Monday morning traffic was busy but moving steadily, and I pulled up just as Mac was getting out of his car. I nodded at him and hustled down to the riverbank.

We stood in the ankle-deep, dewy grass and watched the police dredge the body from the river. It was slow, heavy work. They stood in water over their knees and struggled to free the body from a floating tree limb. The cops had taken off their shoes and rolled up their pants legs in an effort to protect their uniforms, but they were losing the battle. The Arkansas River covered them with water and mud. The body broke free from the limb, and they labored to drag it ashore. They pulled the body out, and it left a long skid mark on the bank of the river. Brown water oozed from the corpse's mouth and nostrils. It was a lousy way for the cops to start the week, and it was worse for the guy who once inhabited the body.

It suddenly struck me that if I hadn't lost a coin toss, I wouldn't be standing there at all. I'd be somewhere else in the city or maybe out in the county, driving dairy products, delivering them to customers, chatting with old friends, and enjoying a spring morning away from life's seamier elements. But I had lost the coin toss, so there I stood. Times were tough for everybody. Take a gander at this poor soul. Six days ago he had forked down a plate of scrambled eggs, swallowed a mug of black coffee, kissed his wife goodbye, and sauntered off to work like a thousand other Joes, except this guy never came back. This guy would never eat another plate of scrambled eggs or drink another cup of coffee. Or kiss his wife goodbye.

"Keep your chin up, Stone," I mumbled to myself. "You haven't got it so bad."

I'd lost the business, and my ex-wife had taken up with a chinchilla rancher in Leoti. Well, hell. I still had my health, didn't I? I was still breathing wasn't I?

"Is this your guy, Stone?"

I leaned over the bloated corpse and choked down the bile rising in my throat. The floater was rank. The Arkansas River slices through the heart of Wichita after tumbling out of the

48

Rockies and crossing the plains. It winds on to the Mississippi River, lifting and carrying debris of life and death along the way.

I stared at the corpse. I knew it was Hamilton. Even through the bloat, I knew it was him. The glasses were gone, swept away in the current no doubt, but a fountain pen was clipped inside his front pocket. Ink had bled over his once white shirt.

McCormick held a handkerchief over his face and pulled a wallet from the dead guy's pocket. It held a few soggy bills, a ten, a five, and two ones, along with a photo of a blonde. I recognized the face in the photograph. It was Lucille Hamilton. He showed me a card that identified its holder as a member of the Institute of the Aeronautical Sciences. The ink had blurred, but the name was still readable, Sidney Hamilton.

"Yeah, that's him," I said.

Another pocket bulged. McCormick pulled out a medicine bottle. The label indicated a prescription for barbiturates. The bottle was empty except for a note. McCormick read it aloud.

To fade away,
only a memory to recall.
To slumber in darkness,
a shadow on the wall.

"What the hell kind of note is this?" McCormick said.

"Damned if I know. Looks like a poem or part of a larger poem, maybe."

Overhead a plane buzzed and banked to the north, disappearing in a cloud beyond the Broadview Hotel. A fat mother goose waddled up the riverbank and scolded a uniformed cop who had come too close to her babies. The cop cordoned off an area around the body. The goose hissed and flapped her wings and slipped into the river with her goslings tucked in a row behind.

"Well, I guess it's a suicide," McCormick said and shook his head. "It's too common these days. He must have taken the barbiturates to muster up enough courage to wade or jump into the river."

I didn't answer. I gazed across the river. Small children, too young for school I guessed, ran in a park. They were filled with that laughter a spring day brings. Behind me morning traffic hummed, and a streetcar clanged.

A uniformed cop walked up.

"Lieutenant McCormick, we found some tire marks in the grass upriver," he said. "Maybe you want to look at them."

Mac nodded, and I followed him. We walked along the bank of the river without speaking until we came to the tire marks. We studied them, but neither of us saw anything that looked out of the ordinary. How could we be sure these tire tracks were linked to Hamilton's death? We couldn't, but when you have little to go on, you grasp at whatever is there.

We walked the few steps from the marks in the grass to the river, staring at the ground like Indian scouts searching a trail. A lone set of footprints in the muddy bank led into the water.

I stared at the ground for several minutes. A dove cooed from over my shoulder. I turned to a gnarled oak tree and saw a brown dove perched on a limb, eyeing me warily. Another dove rested in a nest nearby. I turned back to the footprints and stood closer, measuring the prints against my own.

"Has it rained in the past few days?" I asked McCormick.

"Naw, I don't think so," he said. "Why?"

I stepped back and looked at my prints next to the others.

"No reason," I said, "just wondering."

I walked back toward the marks in the grass. A car had parked on the grassy bank short of the mud along the water's edge. The grass was matted down a bit on one side of the tire marks, probably the driver's side, assuming he drove the car forward to this spot. I stepped to the other side of the tire tracks, where the passenger side of the car would have been and saw matted grass, also. Had someone gotten out of the car on the other side, too? If so, did these tire markings have anything to do with Hamilton and his death? Anyone could have driven to this spot.

"Mac, if these tire marks belong to the Hamilton vehicle, how did the car get downtown where you found it?"

Mac thought for a moment.

"Hamilton drove the car downtown," he said, "after he drove here and scouted the area. It probably took him a while to screw up the courage to kill himself."

"Why would he do that? And how did he get back here?" I said.

"How the hell would I know? Maybe he took a cab. The bus goes by here. Maybe he walked. It's not that far."

"Maybe these tire marks and footprints have nothing to do with Hamilton," I said. "Maybe someone drove to this spot, got out, and went for a swim."

"Maybe," Mac said, "but who goes swimming in his shoes?"

I turned to the footprints leading into the water. Clearly they were made by a man wearing shoes.

"Yeah, right," I said.

I looked toward Central Avenue leading away from the river. This was a fairly busy area. Anybody could have come along and driven to this spot. Maybe somebody stopped here to have a picnic or just gaze at the ducks on the river. Bums, kids, anybody could have stamped down the grass. But how could we explain those footprints leading to the water?

"Why would he drive here first? And why take the car downtown? Why not leave it here?"

"Would you leave your car here?" McCormick said. "This guy may have been a suicide, but he wasn't stupid. He wanted his wife to have the car, safe and unharmed. He drove downtown and parked his car in a lot where he knew it would be found and where he knew it would be safe. I've seen all I need. Let's get back."

We walked back along the river. A number of onlookers milled around the perimeter. We elbowed our way through the throng to where a medical examiner was leaning over the body.

"We figure he went in just up the river," McCormick said. "If he hadn't gotten snagged on those tree limbs along the riverbank, his carcass would've floated halfway to Tulsa by now."

His voice sounded like he wished it had floated down the river, at least out of his jurisdiction. I looked down at the body. Three days ago this guy's wife had come to my office and hired me to find her missing husband. Well, he'd been found, not by me and not the way she had hoped, but that's the way it was. I don't make the rules, and I don't deal the cards. I just play the hand I'm dealt. It was time to cut her in.

McCormick knew he had to deliver the bad news himself, but he didn't want to do it alone. He wanted me to go along.

"You've talked with her, Stone. She's your client. You know her better than I do. Of all the lousy things I have to do in this job, this is the lousiest. I want you to be there."

It was a lousy job, alright, and I wasn't looking forward to it. It was the worst possible news, and of course, Mrs. Hamilton wouldn't take it well. We drove to her place and knocked on the door. She answered it without saying a word. She just looked from McCormick to me and back to McCormick and back to me, again. She knew the verdict.

Her lower lip quivered, her eyes grew wide, and she shook her head from side to side. We led her into her living room. Her shoulders were shaking, and she sobbed into a handkerchief. We sat quietly until she regained control. For several long seconds the only sound in the room was the ticking of the Chelsea clock on the mantel. Finally, she spoke.

"Tell me," she said. "Tell me everything."

Mac told her about the call to the station and Hamilton's body found floating in the river.

"There's no sign of foul play, Mrs. Hamilton. We think your husband committed suicide. We found a note on the body."

Mac reached into his pocket and pulled out the note and handed it to Mrs. Hamilton.

"That's an odd note," he said. "Does is sound like something your husband would write?"

Mrs. Hamilton read the lines but didn't speak.

"Did Mr. Hamilton write poetry?" I asked.

Mrs. Hamilton dabbed at her eyes and nodded.

"Yes, sometimes," she said. "It was just a hobby. He began writing poetry as a release from engineering. He thought writing poetry would be something new, something different from drawing plans. But after he'd done it for several months, he said writing poetry had many similarities to creating a new design. Creating was creating, he said. Poetry and engineering complemented each other."

"We'll have an autopsy performed," Mac said. "It's standard procedure, but it looks like suicide. Had your husband been suffering from stress or depression, Mrs. Hamilton?"

She stopped sobbing long enough to catch her breath and set her jaw.

"My husband did not commit suicide, Lieutenant," she said. "He would never take his own life. I don't know who wrote this note, but it wasn't my husband. If he did write it, it was never intended to be a suicide note. My husband did not commit suicide. Someone murdered my husband."

She was shattered, but she remained resolute. She was frail and tough at the same time. McCormick cleared his throat and dropped his gaze to the floor. He picked at invisible lint on his trousers then looked up.

"Yes, ma'am," he said.

"Do you have any idea why someone would want to kill your husband?" I said.

She dropped her handkerchief from her eyes and her shoulders slumped a little. She shook her head no.

Mrs. Hamilton identified the bottle. She said it belonged to her husband and explained he took the medicine at bedtime.

"His doctor prescribed these. He'd been working hard and had trouble turning off his mind in the evenings. This helped him sleep."

"How long had he been using the medication?" Mac asked.

"Just a few weeks."

"Would you like us to call a neighbor or relative?" I asked.

Mrs. Hamilton stared at a spot in the distance for a long moment. Finally, she said she'd call Alice across the street. We offered our condolences and walked to the door.

We were getting into the car, and I motioned for Mac to hang on. I crossed the street and knocked on the door. When the door opened, I gave Alice Bennett the news.

"I thought it might be better if you heard it from me," I said.

She gasped and clutched the front of her housedress. I asked if she would sit with Mrs. Hamilton, and she said she would.

I got in the car, and McCormick and I drove in silence. There wasn't much to say. Hamilton had been found. My job was over. Case closed or so I thought.

Who knows what demons haunt the soul of another? Who knows what voices visit in the still of the night? Why does the guy who seems to have everything going for him cash in his chips when he's ahead of the game? What makes a man cross over the line, cease resisting, and obey the voices in his head? What? Why?

I'm no head doctor. I've never heard the voices, but Hamilton must have. The only voice I heard said the same thing over and over, "This doesn't add up." The guy had it all, a promising career, a beautiful wife, nice home, bright future. Hell, a million guys would've given an arm to have any one of those things. It didn't add up, and it bothered me.

That night I opened a large volume of the works of William Shakespeare and turned to his comedic play, *As You Like It.* Waldo had identified this play as the source for the mysterious line on Hamilton's clock. I read for an hour or so listening only to the steady ticking of my clocks in the background. When I reached the first scene of Act IV, I found the line I was searching for. It belonged to the character, Rosalind.

"Well, Time is the old justice that examines all such offenders, and let time try: adieu!"

Waldo was right on two accounts. He had not only identified the line from Shakespeare's work, but he'd noted that the quote I'd given him, "Time is the justice that examines all offenders," was not an exact quote. It appeared Hamilton had taken some poetic license with his Shakespeare. I finished reading the play and closed the volume and went to bed.

Thursday, April 29

I wasn't surprised when Mrs. Hamilton showed up in my office the day after her husband's funeral. It was a gray day, threatening rain. We needed it. I had my feet up on my desk, and I was reading the sports page. The Philadelphia Phillies had won a pair against the Boston Bees, and the Athletics had taken care of the Senators. I mused that it was a good day to be from the city of brotherly love when she walked in.

I folded the paper and stood up. I offered her my condolences again as she took a chair. She nodded her gratitude and jumped right in.

"Mr. Stone, I want you to find my husband's murderer," she said.

She was grieving, but she had fire in her eyes. I didn't answer right away. I offered her a cigarette and lit it along with one for myself.

"I was afraid you might," I said, "but frankly, Mrs. Hamilton, I'd recommend against it. A suicide is difficult to accept. It's difficult for anyone, and denying the evidence is perfectly normal. Still, the evidence suggests your husband took his own life. There's no indication that he was murdered."

She listened silently then looked at me with fiery eyes.

"My husband did not commit suicide, Mr. Stone," she said. "I don't give a damn about the evidence. He did not do it."

I didn't speak.

"He loved me," she said. "He loved his life. He loved his career. Maybe my reaction to this is expected. It's called denial, I suppose. I don't care what it's called. I know Sidney…"

She caught herself.

"I knew my husband," she said. "He did not commit suicide."

Again, I didn't speak. Several seconds passed, our eyes met, and hers never wavered. I glanced down at my shoes and looked back up. Suddenly her eyes grew wide.

"You don't think he took his own life either, do you?" she said. "Do you?"

I fidgeted and glanced at the ceiling. She deserved a straight answer.

"Mrs. Hamilton, I didn't know your husband. There's no way for me to know or understand what happened. I'll admit I have my doubts, but that's all I have, doubts, a gut feeling and nothing else. There isn't a shred of evidence to suggest your husband was murdered."

"That's fine," she said. "I'll take whatever you've got, even if it's only doubts. That's a start. I'll leave it up to you to find the evidence."

"Mrs. Hamilton," I said, "I think you'll be wasting your money. I have to be honest."

"It's my money," she said, "and I wish to use it to hire your time. I wish to hire your gut instinct. Will you do it, Mr. Stone?"

She was determined, and she wouldn't take no for an answer. I admired the woman's resolve. Her steady gaze never left mine.

"Yes, Mrs. Hamilton," I said, "I'll see what I can do."

She shook my hand, and just like that I was back in business.

I didn't know where else to start so I decided to go back to the beginning, to the river. I stood on the grass above the muddy bank where the sweaty cops had pulled the body out of the water. I walked down to the water's edge and looked over the gnarled branch that had snagged the body and kept it from floating to Oklahoma. The gray, bare limb lay on the bank caked with dried mud. A bumblebee hovered over the limb, lighted for a brief moment, and buzzed away toward more promising prospects. I didn't blame it.

I looked more closely at the limb, and noticed something fluttering on the end of a twig. I snapped off the twig and studied what appeared to be a small piece of cloth. I pulled it off and rinsed it in the water, and although it was muddy and gray, I figured it must have been a small piece of Hamilton's once-white shirt, torn off when the cops dragged his body ashore.

After a few moments, I started walking upriver. I felt a bit like that bumblebee, zigzagging from point to point, blindly searching, and blissfully unaware that its flight flouted the rules of nature. I came to the tire tread marks in the grass and the footprints in the mud. The footprints still led to the river. Once again, I stood next to the prints and tried to figure out why they bothered me. Then it hit me. Although the prints were about the same size as mine, they were deeper, made by a heavier man. I pulled a photograph of Hamilton out of my pocket and studied it. Hamilton hadn't been a big man. In fact, he had a slighter build than I did. I looked at the footprints again and knew they didn't belong to Hamilton. Were they made by a heavier man or were they made by one man carrying another?

I stashed the picture back in my pocket and walked down to the water's edge. There was a slight ridge of mud along the water at the foot of the bank. I took off my shoes and socks and tossed them onto the grass above. I rolled up my pants legs and crept downriver along the ridge, keeping my balance with my left hand on the bank.

I'd gone a short ways, twenty steps or so, when I approached a cedar tree growing near the edge of the bank. A needled limb hung out over the water. A fat goose squatted beneath the limb. As I drew closer, the goose eyed me warily, and when I got too close it squawked at my rudeness and waddled further down the bank before slipping into the water and paddling away.

There it was. There on that muddy ridge where the goose had been lying beneath the cedar limb was what I had been looking for, even though I didn't know what I was looking for until I saw it. There in the mud was another set of footprints, similar to the ones twenty steps upriver. Except these prints were a bit shallower, and these prints led out of the water.

It was a little before noon. I sat in my office looking over my notes and forming a bare bones outline of Hamilton's life in my mind. I was going over the materials Mrs. Hamilton had given me, mostly photos of the young newly-wed couple. The pictures were of the usual stuff — enjoying a picnic, sitting by a lake, holiday dinners with parents.

The photos were more numerous during the early years of their marriage and had grown fewer in number in recent years. Why was that? People seem to take lots of pictures when they are young and newly married and again right after a baby is born, but then the ordinariness of life sets in, and the interest in recording it trails off. How many pictures do people take of their adolescent children? People seem to be fascinated with things that are new, but our interest wanes quickly.

I looked at one photo that appeared to be a Thanksgiving dinner. There were about a dozen people seated around the table with the Hamiltons, probably parents and siblings, maybe cousins.

I leaned back and closed my eyes and thought for a few moments. I opened the yearbook and turned to the page with the photo of the Engineering Society. There was a smiling Sidney Hamilton, and next to him was James Ireland. I turned to the pages with the German club and the chess club, and James Ireland was in each photograph. I thumbed back through the pages I'd already looked at and noticed how much alike the two men appeared. Hamilton was a bit darker, more confident looking, perhaps. They didn't look exactly alike, not like twins, but they had similarities. They could easily pass as brothers. They looked like they dressed from the same closet of clothes.

I made a note to call Ireland, but first I wanted to talk to Hamilton's boss at Stearman. I didn't know if he would be available or if he was off on another jaunt, but I was going to talk to him. The rest of my plan was pretty fuzzy as are most of my plans. Usually I stumble around peeking into doors and peering into closets until something turns up. Maybe I discover a clue or maybe I rattle someone with something to hide into bolting from cover. Something usually happens. It's not very efficient, and it's damned sure not scientific, but it works for me.

Meeting with Hamilton's boss turned out to be easier than I thought. My phone rang, and I answered it.

"Stone Investigations."

"Is this Mr. Stone?"

The voice was female.

"Yes, speaking."

"Mr. Stone, this is Mrs. Richeson, secretary to Mr. Gordon Veatch. I'm calling from Stearman Aircraft."

"Hello, Mrs. Richeson, how can I help you?"

"Mr. Stone, Mr. Veatch would like to speak with you regarding the late Mr. Hamilton. He was wondering if you'd be available to meet with him in his office."

Would I meet with him? Hell yes, I'd meet with him, but why was he calling me?

"I think I could manage that, Mrs. Richeson. When did he have in mind?"

"As soon as possible, please. Could you come by this afternoon, say two o'clock?"

I paused as if checking my calendar.

"Yes, that would be fine," I said.

She gave me an address on South Oliver and rang off. Now what was this about? When I called before, Veatch was unavailable, now he suddenly wanted to meet with me. I wouldn't have long to wonder. I looked at my watch and saw that it was just after twelve-thirty. I decided to grab a bite to eat at the Eaton Hotel before heading for his office. An hour later I was heading south on Oliver Street.

The day had turned pleasant, and the threat of rain had dissipated. Like I said before, Wichita weather is fickle. I was driving with the top down on my car enjoying the spring air.

I drive a Jones Six Sports Roadster that's worth more than I could afford to pay. I received the car a couple of years ago as payment from a client for services rendered. The client had asked me to recover some stolen property, some uninsured jewelry heisted from a wall safe in his home. I checked with McCormick and learned that he and his men had been working for some time to bring down a cat burglar in the area, but the trail had gone cold. The burglar had moved out of Mac's jurisdiction.

Clues to his whereabouts pointed to the southwest, and by the time I caught up with him, I was in L.A. I reported to the L.A. police and got a fix on the burglar's M.O. and staked out likely targets until he appeared. I caught the burglar and recovered a great deal of jewelry and cash. The police departments in both

L.A. and Wichita were grateful, never a bad thing for a private detective.

Some of my client's jewelry had been sold, but much of it was recovered, and he was grateful, too. He offered me some handsome pieces of jewelry as payment for my services, but what would a guy like me do with fancy diamonds? So instead, he handed me the keys to the roadster. Of course I protested. It had been a long case, and my expenses had run high, but the car was worth much more than my fee. He wouldn't relent, however, and the roadster became mine.

The Jones Motor Car Company built cars in Wichita from 1914 to 1920, before a fire destroyed much of their business. They never recovered which was unfortunate. The company built a fine automobile, and the roadster was a wonderful car. I've enjoyed driving mine every day I've owned it. It's a convertible, and it seats four comfortably, plenty big for me. It pleased me to own something that was not only well-crafted but unique.

I pulled up at the address on South Oliver and parked. The building looked simple and functional. In the distance I spotted a runway and a hangar. A windsock indicated a stiff breeze out of the south. Several bright yellow and blue biplanes rested on the runway, and several more were clustered in the hangar. I recognized them as Model 75 Kaydets, military aircraft trainers. Mechanics and production personnel worked together on the aircraft. I noticed a couple of similar planes buzzing overhead.

I stepped into the offices and introduced myself to a woman seated at a desk. She stood up as soon as I came in.

"I'm Mrs. Richeson, Mr. Stone. Please come with me. Mr. Veatch asked me not to keep you waiting."

She led me down a hallway lined with photographs on the walls of aircraft and the men who created them. She knocked quietly on a door and opened it.

"Mr. Veatch, this is Mr. Stone," she said, addressing a man seated at a drafting table. He was looking over some blueprints. I didn't see her leave, but I heard the door close behind me. The man at the table stood up and extended his hand. I shook it.

"I'm Gordon Veatch, Mr. Stone. Please have a seat," he said, indicating a chair in front of his desk. Veatch was short and stocky and looked like he was accustomed to throwing his ample weight around. He wore shirtsleeves and a tie and a pair of gold wire-rimmed glasses. He took the overstuffed chair behind the desk.

"Pleased to meet you, Mr. Veatch," I said, "but I confess I was surprised when your secretary called."

He sat back in his chair, folded his hands beneath his double chin, and pursed his lips.

"Yes, well, as you know, Mr. Stone, we here at Stearman Aircraft have suffered a crushing blow with the death of one of our brightest engineers. We are going to miss Sidney Hamilton very much."

"Yes, I read about that in the papers. A tragic loss," I said.

Veatch raised his eyebrows and placed his hands on his desk. He leaned forward slightly.

"Please don't toy with me, Mr. Stone. I'm not stupid, and I have no patience with those who are. I've spoken to Lucille Hamilton. I know she asked you to investigate the case of her husband's suicide. She thinks it was murder, and she wants you to find this murderer. Isn't that right, Mr. Stone? Well, listen to me. There was no murder. The police have declared his death a suicide. I abhor your principles, Mr. Stone, and frankly, your actions are reprehensible. You are taking advantage of a grieving widow who is not thinking clearly at the moment. I've asked you here today to insist that you stop your silly investigation and leave that poor woman alone."

I leaned back in my chair and looked across the desk. Veatch was a man who was used to speaking in a superior tone and expected his wishes to be obeyed.

"I see. Well, obviously I don't agree with you, Mr. Veatch, but let's suppose for a minute that you are correct. Let's suppose I have no principles, and I am taking advantage of a grieving widow. What business is it of yours?"

Veatch's face reddened, but his voice remained calm.

"We are a small, growing company made up of loyal and dedicated people," he said. "We care for our employees and their families."

Small company or not, private lives should remain private, I thought, but I decided not to voice my opinion.

"Mr. Veatch, I don't know yet whether Sidney Hamilton was murdered or committed suicide, but I intend to find out. What was he working on when he died? Was it a special project of some sort? James Ireland thought he'd been under a lot of stress."

Veatch looked apoplectic.

"James Ireland? What does he have to do with this? What has he said to you?"

Of course, James Ireland had said no such thing. I was just fishing. Veatch's face grew darker.

"I'm not about to discuss our company's business with a down-at-the-heels gumshoe," he said.

I glanced at my heels of my shoes. Veatch's appraisal seemed a bit harsh.

"Can you tell me why he parked downtown every day for the last several weeks before he died? Why wasn't he coming to your offices here?" I asked.

This brought him to the boiling point.

"Mr. Stone, I must ask you to leave, but before you go, I am going to say this one more time. Drop this case."

"That sounds dangerously close to a threat," I said.

"Take it as you will, Mr. Stone. I want you off this case."

"This case involves the death of a man, a man who worked for you. I would think you'd want some answers. I would think you'd want the truth."

"I have all the answers I need," he said. "The police have ruled it a suicide. That's what it is."

"Hamilton's death probably was a suicide. On the other hand, it may have been a murder. Either way, as I said earlier, I intend to find out, and until I do find out, there's one thing you should remember. I work for my client, and I answer only to my client."

Gordon Veatch looked like he might explode. I figured he seldom heard anyone talk back to him. He looked like a man who was used to hearing "yes sir" a lot. I stood up and moved toward the door. Before I opened it I turned to Veatch.

"I have just one more question," I said. "Did you or one of your people leave a pile of crushed rocks in the seat of my car?"

Veatch didn't speak. He just opened and closed his mouth. He looked at me like I was a lunatic. Who knows? Maybe he was right.

I sat in my office and tried to make sense of my meeting with Gordon Veatch. What had it been about? Why was Hamilton's former boss so adamant that I drop the case? Was he trying to hide something? If there were questions about Hamilton's death, wouldn't Veatch want answers, too? Why was he threatened by my association with Mrs. Hamilton? I didn't believe it was mere concern for her well-being. Something about his concern for her welfare seemed as phony as a three dollar bill. I had lots of questions and no answers. I felt like a hell of a detective.

I looked at my watch. It was nearly four o'clock. I dialed the number James Ireland had given me. He answered on the third ring.

"Mr. Ireland, this is Pete Stone. I wondered if I might meet with you concerning the death of Mr. Hamilton."

There was a brief moment of silence.

"I guess I've been expecting you to call. Lucille told me she was going to ask you to continue the investigation. I must be frank, Mr. Stone. I advised Lucille not to hire you. She is not well. She is distraught and not thinking clearly. The sooner she accepts Sidney's death and moves on, the sooner she'll get over the pain."

"I'm surprised to hear you say that, Mr. Ireland. I would think that you'd want to eliminate any doubt in the death of your best friend."

"I have no doubt, Mr. Stone. The police have investigated Sidney's death and ruled it a suicide. I have to accept it, too, as painful as it is."

"Will you meet with me?"

There was another pause.

"Yes, I'll meet with you, but only very briefly. If Mr. Veatch finds out I've seen you, he'll fire me. He was very clear about that. He just called me. He's already upset that I spoke to you last Saturday. He doesn't care for you very much, Mr. Stone."

"Imagine my dismay. So why are you willing to meet with me?"

"It's the least I can do for my best friend. If there is the slightest doubt this was a suicide, I'd like to help."

Ireland suggested we meet in thirty minutes at a small café on Mead Street a block north of Douglas. I said that would be fine and hung up. It took a few minutes to straighten up my desk and lock the door. Mead is only a few blocks from my office, so I decided to walk.

I looked at my watch when I arrived and saw that I was a few minutes early. I took a booth in the back. I ordered a cup of coffee and lit a cigarette. The café did most of its trade at lunchtime, and it was quiet at this time of day. I looked out the window and watched the traffic on Mead and Douglas. Across Douglas I could see Milton's parking lot, and Milton was busy helping late afternoon customers get to their cars and exit the lot.

After a few minutes, Ireland entered the café, nodded at me, and slid into the other side of the booth.

"Thanks for meeting with me, Mr. Ireland."

"It's the least I can do. I do care for Lucille. I don't agree with her, but I do care for her."

I nodded. The waitress arrived, and Ireland ordered coffee with cream. I waited until she returned with the coffee before speaking.

"The police have ruled Mr. Hamilton's death a suicide, and you seem convinced they are correct. Hamilton was your best friend. Weren't you surprised that he killed himself?"

Ireland lit a cigarette and nodded.

"Of course I was surprised. I wish I had seen it coming."

"Why didn't you?"

Ireland looked startled.

"I'm sorry," I said. "That was pretty blunt. What I meant was people who commit suicide generally telegraph their intentions in advance. Sometimes there are obvious signs of depression, sometimes they get their affairs in order, sometimes they ask for help and no one listens. I'm surprised that your best friend was able to hide his intentions so carefully from both his wife and his best friend."

"I understand your thinking, Mr. Stone, but you didn't know Sidney. I knew him most of my life. He could be very stoical. He kept his pain and his troubles to himself. I doubt if he ever told Lucille everything he felt. It simply wasn't in his nature to complain."

"Let's assume for a moment that the police are correct," I said. "Let's assume Mr. Hamilton did commit suicide. Why would he have done such a thing? It looks to me like he had a good life with a bright future."

Ireland sipped his coffee and nodded. The waitress arrived to refill our cups.

"Yes, he did have a bright future. Sidney was very intelligent, and he was held in high regard at Stearman."

Ireland paused for a moment and looked over his shoulder. A couple of city workers were sitting at the counter. Except for them and the waitress and the cook, we were the only people in the café. Ireland turned back to me.

"Look, Mr. Stone, I can't go into any details. I shouldn't even mention this, but Sidney was under pressure, a lot of pressure."

I didn't say anything. There's nothing like silence to get someone to talk. Ireland squirmed. He looked over his shoulder again.

"I can't talk about this."

"Are you worried about Veatch?"

Ireland shook his head like he was talking to a moron.

"Oh, this is much bigger than Veatch. Veatch would fire me, sure. But other people would do worse, much worse."

I leaned forward.

"Do you mean to tell me that you are in danger for talking to me? Was Mr. Hamilton in danger? Why haven't you said anything before?"

Ireland held up his hands.

"Wait a minute. Wait a minute. I never said Sidney was in danger. I said Sidney was under pressure, tremendous pressure. I think he cracked under the strain."

Something smelled like day old fish.

"Why the pressure?"

"I told you, Mr. Stone, I can't talk about this."

He crushed out his cigarette and stood up.

"Look, I have to leave now. I have to warn you I'm going to suggest to Lucille that she divest herself of your services at once. Sidney died at his own hand, and picking at the open wound will not bring him back. It could even be dangerous. Good afternoon, Mr. Stone."

He turned on his heel and left. I tossed some money on the table and went to the door. It was well after five o'clock, and the shadows were growing long. The streets and walks were busy with people going home. Ireland walked south to Douglas Street. At the corner he turned right. I put my hat down low and followed him. When I reached the corner, I saw him about a half a block ahead and watched him disappear in a doorway. I walked quickly and stopped at the doorway. It was the entrance to an unassuming brick structure two stories high. There was no name on the building.

I stepped back and saw a light come on in a second story window. I crossed Douglas so I could look back and get a better view. After about a quarter of an hour the light went off, and a few moments later Ireland came out. He crossed Douglas heading right for me, so I turned toward a shop window and pretended to be interested in a typewriter on display. Ireland didn't notice me and began walking east on the sidewalk. I followed for a couple of blocks and watched him turn in at Milton's parking lot.

"I'll be damned," I whispered.

In a few minutes, Ireland reappeared driving a late model Ford. He turned east on Douglas and disappeared in the traffic. I walked back to the building he had entered and noted its address in my book. Traffic was still heavy. I wanted to see what was in that building, but I would have to wait until things were quieter.

I sat on a barstool in Tom's Inn sipping on a Storz draft beer and considered my options. Tom had the radio on above the bar. The Cardinals were in Chicago getting pounded by the Cubs, 8 to 2. I knew the feeling.

A smart guy would leave the investigation alone. Ireland said that Hamilton was under a lot of pressure, and the pressure got to him. He said Hamilton committed suicide. The cops agreed. Everyone agreed, except for Mrs. Hamilton. I wasn't sure either. I could give up or I could continue bumbling along in my usual fashion, sneaking through doors and beating my head against walls until something turned up, if anything ever did. It was a hell of a choice. I took another sip of beer and smiled. I knew what I would do. I knew I would keep looking, but then again, no one ever accused me of being a smart guy.

A man sat down next to me and ordered a Storz draft, also. Tom pulled the stick and filled a frosty mug. He put the beer in front of him, and the guy took a long pull.

"Say, that's good," he said.

I agreed, and he nodded. The guy was big. A lot of other adjectives would describe him, but none fit better than 'big.' His shoulders looked like they could lift a Chevy and probably had. This was a guy who used his brawn, who moved heavy things. He had forearms the size of my calves with tattoos on each of them. The one on the left read "Born to Kill." The one on the right read "Mom." Mr. Tough Guy and Mr. Sensitive, a real complex character.

The door opened, and a woman came in. She'd seen better days. At least I hoped she had, but her better days were in the rear view mirror. She wore a long, dirty overcoat that came to her ankles. The weather was mild, but I figured her coat was also her mattress. Her hair was stringy, and she carried a shopping bag that probably held all her worldly belongings. She stood in the doorway and let her eyes adjust to the dim lighting before shuffling to the empty barstool on the other side of Mr. Big.

"A glass of water, please," she said.

Tom filled a glass with water and set it on the bar in front of her.

71

"Anything else?" he said.

She looked around the bar at the patrons who were drinking, eating, and chatting. Her tongue touched her lips.

"No," she said.

The big guy raised his empty mug, and I did the same. Tom filled them both.

"Jesus, Tom," the big guy said, "can't you control the clientele in here? Something stinks. Do I have to sit next to trash?"

If he'd left it at that, it might have stopped there, but he didn't, and it didn't.

"A guy comes into a tavern to have a beer, he shouldn't have to sit next to trash," he mumbled, loud enough to be heard by most of the patrons. Heads turned in his direction. I stared at a point directly in front of me.

"That's enough," I said. "You've made your point."

The big guy swiveled his stool in my direction. I continued looking straight ahead.

"What'd you say, mister?"

"You heard me. Leave it alone."

"Suppose you make me?" he said.

Great. Big and tough, just what I needed. I knew I couldn't go toe-to-toe with this mountain. He'd crush me like a brittle twig. I was pretty sure he knew that, too.

"I don't suppose we could just drop this, could we?" I said. "Just drink our beers and forget it?"

"Not a chance," he said.

"I didn't think so," I said.

I came up fast with my elbow and caught him flush on the nose. It knocked him back a little, but he remained on his stool. I followed with a kick to the side of his knee and heard a crack. He yelped and swung at me with a wild haymaker. I ducked and slid off my stool. He turned on his stool, but his size slowed him down. I hit him with a right cross on his left ear and followed with a left to the chin and repeated the combination. His eyes became unfocused, and he slid off the stool and sat dazed on the floor. The bar had grown quiet. Patrons had stopped to watch the excitement.

In a few seconds his head started to clear, and he looked around the room. His right hand inched to an inside pocket of his jacket. I didn't know what he had in there, and I didn't intend to find out.

"You have two choices," I said. "You can keep reaching for whatever you're packing, in which case I'll draw my gun and shoot you or you can get up and leave and live to fight another day."

He thought for a minute. I figured on a good day he didn't think quickly, and this wasn't a good day. His hand stopped moving, and with a huge grunt he pulled himself to his feet. He'd lifted heavy weight all his life, but he probably wasn't used to lifting himself off the floor. He stood for a moment. Maybe he was reconsidering his options, but he slowly turned toward the door. I don't know why, but I suddenly felt sorry for him. He was big and dumb, but where's the crime in that?

"There's a third option," I said, "but it would take a big man to choose it."

He turned around and faced me.

"Yeah, what's that?"

"You could apologize to the lady here, shake my hand, and let me buy you a beer."

I heard a few mumblings from the other patrons.

"You just kicked my ass," he said. "Not many guys ever done that."

"No, I don't suppose they have," I said.

"Anybody ever kick your ass?"

"Yes," I said.

"Not many, I'll bet."

"No, not many."

He nodded his head and turned to the woman on the barstool.

"Ma'am, I apologize for the remarks I made. I was wrong, and I'm sorry."

The woman nodded, and the big guy turned to me. He stuck out a huge paw. I took it and we shook.

"Tom, how about a couple of beers," I said.

We sat back down and clinked our mugs together. The rest of the people in the tavern went back to what they were doing. Mabel was standing in the doorway of the kitchen, and I caught her eye and gave her a signal. In a few moments a roast beef sandwich and a beer appeared in front of the woman in the overcoat.

The big guy turned out to be okay. His name was Leonard, and he was a little slow, and he tended to let his muscles do the talking, but he was a decent guy. He liked baseball, and he hated the Yankees so he couldn't be all bad. We drank our beers and chatted about baseball and nothing else in particular. The Cubs finally finished off the Cardinals, 11 to 3. The world continued to spin on its axis. I thought about changing my business cards to read "Pete Stone, Righter of Wrongs."

I mulled over my meeting with James Ireland. Did he have an office in the building downtown? Had Hamilton had an office there also? Was Ireland in the same office? If so, that would explain Ireland's parking in Milton's lot, but it didn't explain why the office existed, and it didn't explain all the secrecy. I intended to find out. I finished my beer and followed with a couple more, sipping slowly and smoking cigarettes. One thing this job demands is patience. Being a detective means being slow and deliberate, long hours of boredom interspersed with moments of intense action. You could say the same thing about being a fireman, I suppose.

The crowd had thinned somewhat, although the place was still jumping. The big guy, Leonard, had called it a night. The lady in the coat had left, also. I hoped she had someplace better to go than the city park, but I doubted it.

I dropped some money on the bar and gave both Tom and Mabel a wave goodbye. I drove back downtown and was pleased to see how quiet it was. It was nearing midnight. An occasional pedestrian still strolled on the walks, and I was pleased with that. I didn't want to be noticed, but I didn't want to look suspicious either. If the streets and walks were empty and a cop spotted me, I might have to explain what I was doing. I didn't want to do that, because my plan was to force my way into Ireland's office. It's called breaking and entering, B&E for short.

I parked on Douglas Avenue across from Ireland's building and looked both ways as I approached the entryway. I tried the door, and it was locked. The upper half of the door was glass, and I could see a night watchman sitting at a desk in the foyer, reading a newspaper. I checked the lock. It used a simple skeleton key which wouldn't be difficult to pick. The building's tenants counted on the watchman to maintain security. I'd have no trouble picking the lock, but I'd have to get past the watchman.

I crossed the street and got back in my car. I rolled it back a few feet to where I could get a better angle of sight into the foyer and see the watchman. I reached under the front seat of my car and pulled out a small box of tools. Then I lit a cigarette and leaned back and waited.

I've mentioned before that a guy who can't wait wouldn't last long in this job. Most guys in this business have tricks to keep them alert while they wait. I liked to think, to recall something from the past and go over it, remembering the details. Sometimes I thought about sex. Okay, oftentimes I thought about sex. Sometimes I thought about food, savoring the memory of a particularly good meal I had eaten. This night, I thought about baseball. I thought about last season's New York Yankees and wondered if anybody could beat them this year. They had the big names, guys like Gehrig and Dickey and Crosetti. That new kid, DiMaggio, looked good, too. It was always tough to beat the Yankees.

I smoked another cigarette then another and another. After close to an hour, the watchman put down the paper and stood up. I grabbed my tools and got out of the car. I watched him look at a clock and walk away from the desk. I didn't know if this was a scheduled round to check the building or a nature call, but this was my chance to get in the building. As soon as he disappeared from the foyer I went to work on the door. It took less than a minute to open the lock and get through the door. Thankfully, there was little pedestrian traffic.

I went straight up the stairs listening for sounds of the watchman. At the top of the stairs I peeked around the corner and saw the hall was empty. I went to the office I had marked from the street, and of course the door was locked. This one had a deadbolt that required a bit more skill to open. I worked as fast and as quietly as I could. The bolt clicked to the side, and I was in.

I closed the door and turned on a light. The office itself wasn't much. It was small and probably served only one person, James Ireland. There was a desk and a chair, but no chair for a visitor. On the desk sat a phone, an empty in/out basket, a notepad, and a few pencils. The notepad had a blank sheet of paper on top. I tore it off and put it in my pocket.

Next to the desk were a drafting table and a stool. Plans were spread over the table. They seemed to be for a telescopic device of some sort, but I didn't understand them. Being a super sleuth, I figured the plans had something to do with the aircraft industry. I tried to read the notations on the plans and discovered they weren't written in English. The notations appeared to be written in German.

I tore another page from Ireland's notepad to write down the notations and have them translated later. I never got it done. I heard a slight rustle behind me and started to turn, but before I did something cold and metallic was pressed against the side of my head.

"Make one move, and it'll be your last," a voice said.

I thought the voice sounded a bit dramatic, but the gun barrel against my head was cold and real. I didn't move.

We were only a few blocks from police headquarters. It didn't take long for two uniformed cops to arrive and cuff me. I'd never seen one of them, but the other one I recalled from the river. He'd helped haul Hamilton's body out of the water. He nodded in a crisp, business-like manner and led me to the patrol car. Minutes later I was turned over to a desk sergeant for processing.

"I'd like to speak to Lieutenant McCormick," I said.

"It'll have to wait till morning," the sergeant said. "The lieutenant is off for the night. In the meantime, we have a nice, comfy room waiting for you."

The desk sergeant grinned and motioned for the uniforms to take me away. I wasn't optimistic about the room being either nice or comfy, and my pessimism was justified. The cell was dimly lit and it stank of urine. I sat down on the cot and listened to the cell door slam shut. There's something about the sound of slamming bars on a jail cell that sends chills up the spines of the strongest men. Grown men, real tough guys, have been known to cry out for their mommas when they hear that sound.

I sat on the cot for a moment and let my eyes adjust to the dim light. After a few moments I lay down and faced the wall. I noticed I wasn't alone. A huge cockroach crawled on the cinderblocks about six inches from my nose. When it got to eye level it stopped and twitched its antennae. I stared at it without moving, and it twitched again and stared back at me. We held our respective positions for several beats. Neither of us moved. Finally, it grew bored and moved on. I had won. I had stared down a cockroach. Some victory. I didn't feel much like a winner.

The light was too dim to see much else, so I called out.

"Hey, is anybody there?"

Voices came back at me.

"Shut up!"

"Go to sleep, asshole."

"Keep it down."

Presumably, there were other guests in the crowbar hotel. I noticed a sink and a toilet in the corner of my cell. I staggered to the corner and relieved myself in the toilet. The sink was filthy, but I managed to wash my hands and face. I shuffled back to the cot, whispered goodnight to the cockroach, and drifted off to sleep.

Friday, April 30

I was awakened in the morning by clanging bars and voices clamoring for breakfast. I was stiff and sore. I wasn't hungry, but I needed a cigarette and coffee more than my next breath. I didn't have either, so I sat up and kept breathing. I heard footsteps followed by a voice. The voice belonged to Lieutenant McCormick. The bars slid back, and he came into the cell and stood over me.

"Jesus, Stone, you look like hell."

"That makes sense. I feel like hell. It's a package."

A deputy was with Mac, standing a few paces behind him. I sat up on the cot.

"Well, you've really screwed yourself this time, Stone," Mac said. "What the hell were you thinking? You've pissed off some pretty important people. You'll probably lose your license, and you may do some time."

"Aren't you the bearer of good news?" I said. "Have you got a cigarette?"

He did, and he gave me one. I inhaled deeply.

"Anything else?" I said.

"Yeah, somebody named Veatch wants you put away. He's some big hotshot at Stearman Aircraft."

I nodded.

"Yeah, I've met him," I said.

Mac grinned.

"Well, that would explain why he hates you, I guess. You need to work on your manners, Stone. What's up with you? Why did you break into one of their offices? I've got a night watchman who claims he caught you red-handed. Veatch claims you were stealing top secret plans. Veatch says you're a threat to the security of the United States of America. I think I agree with him. I know you're a threat to Wichita. This has something to do with that Hamilton suicide, doesn't it?"

I nodded again. My head still hurt.

"I'm on to something, Mac. I don't know what yet, but I'm on to something. I followed one of Stearman's engineers to that office, a guy who works for Veatch. The guy also happened to be Hamilton's best friend."

"So you followed a guy? So what? Why does that give you the right to commit B&E? You're acting like a rookie, Stone. You ever hear of getting a warrant?"

"A judge wouldn't have given me a warrant. I have no evidence. I'm working on a hunch."

Mac shook his head in disgust.

"You and your hunches," he said. "Well, you'll have a chance to explain it to the judge. Veatch is pressing charges. He wants your ass in a sling. I think he's got it, too. You'd better get a lawyer."

"And in the meantime?"

"In the meantime," Mac said, "you'll post bond and be free to go, but don't leave town. Get a lawyer, stay close, and watch your step. If you screw up again before your trial, you'll be back in the slammer."

"Thanks, Mac. I owe you."

Mac grinned.

"You're damn right you owe me. You can pay me back at Christmas."

I nodded. Christmas would be coming in the spring this year. I left the police station and stood on the steps outside. I breathed in a lungful of clean air. I walked down the steps to the sidewalk shaking the stiffness out of my bones.

Fortunately, I was only a few blocks from where I'd parked my car the night before. As I walked, I considered my situation, and it wasn't good. Mac was right. I had screwed up. I was in trouble. I was going to go to trial, and since I was considered a threat to the security of the country, I would probably lose my license and my livelihood.

I had a lot on my mind, but my head was too fuzzy to think clearly. What I needed now was a shower, coffee, and breakfast, pretty much in that order. I'd sort out the rest later.

I drove home to clean up. When I emptied my pockets, the slip of paper I'd torn off Ireland's notepad fell out. I held it up to the light where I could make out some scratches. The scratches looked like the impression of a name and a phone number. I put the paper on the table and lightly ran the tip of a lead pencil over it. The impression became more visible. It was a name and number. I wrote them down in my book and tossed the paper in the trash.

I took a hot shower and drove over to the Broadview for breakfast. I was hungry, and I had an ulterior motive. I planned on asking Agnes to go on a date with me this evening. From the way Mac talked, I might not have much more time as a free man. I might as well enjoy what freedom I had. The Gage Brewer band was playing at the Kaliko Kat, and I intended to ask Agnes to join me for dinner and drinks.

I took a table in the restaurant and lit a cigarette. A waitress came over and poured coffee.

"Is Agnes around?" I asked.

The waitress didn't say anything. She just shook her head and moved to another table. When the waitress returned, I ordered ham and eggs. I tried to get her to talk.

"Listen, I thought Agnes would be working today," I said. "I was hoping to speak to her. What's up? Is she sick or something?"

The waitress looked back over her shoulder toward the kitchen.

"I can't say," she said. "You'll have to ask the manager."

She disappeared into the kitchen. I lit another cigarette and drank my coffee. A group of four businessmen sat at a nearby table. Across the room at a larger table were a number of women. They looked like they might belong to a club of some sort, and their conversation was animated and sprinkled with laughter. I turned around and looked back into the lobby. The shoeshine stand was empty. Ellis Waldo wasn't around.

The waitress returned with my ham and eggs. She slipped a note under my plate and winked at me before she walked away. The restaurant manager came out of the kitchen and walked toward my table. I palmed the note and put it in my pocket as he reached my table.

"I understand you've been asking about Agnes," he said.

I nodded.

"That's right. I was wondering why she's not working this morning."

"Agnes doesn't work here anymore," he said.

I raised my eyebrows.

"Really? I'm surprised. When did she quit?"

"She didn't quit," he said. "She was fired."

"Fired? What for?" I asked.

"Not that it's any of your business, but I fired her for serving that nigger."

The manager jutted his chin in the direction of the shoeshine stand. The businessmen at the next table looked in our direction.

"I warned her more than once," he said, "but she kept bringing him in here."

I didn't say anything. I stood up.

"Where are you going?" he asked.

"I've lost my appetite," I said.

The businessmen had halted their conversation. They turned toward my table.

"You can't just walk out of here without paying," he said. "You owe me for this breakfast."

I picked up the plate of ham and eggs and smashed it into his face.

"You eat it," I said.

The manager sputtered and fell backwards. The businessmen were grinning. The women at the large table were watching, too. I heard mumblings and a couple of "oh, dears." I walked out of the restaurant.

Not bad, Stone, I thought to myself. You've been out of jail for nearly two hours, and already you've tangled with someone else. Mac may have been on to something when he questioned my manners.

I drove to my office and sat behind my desk. I pulled the waitress's note out of my pocket. She'd written Agnes's name and a phone number on it. I tried the number. Agnes answered on the second ring. I told her what had happened at the Broadview, and she giggled like a schoolgirl. We chatted for a few minutes, and I told her I'd like to take her out this evening. She was excited and agreed that I'd pick her up at her place.

"Thanks for calling, Pete," she said. "Your timing is perfect. I could really use a night on the town."

"Me, too, kiddo," I said and rang off.

I made another call, this one to Mrs. Hamilton. As soon as I told her who was calling, I could hear the concern in her voice.

"Oh, Mr. Stone, I just spoke to Mr. Veatch. I feel just terrible. I never wanted to cause this much trouble. Mr. Veatch is awfully angry with you, and he can be a frightening man. I'm so sorry."

"Don't worry, Mrs. Hamilton," I said. "I often make people angry. It comes with the job. I'm pretty good at it, actually."

"Yes, well, that may be," she said, "but you don't know Mr. Veatch. He's a very powerful man. Mr. Stone, please take care of yourself."

I told her again not to worry and assured her I would continue with the case, and we hung up. I remembered the number I had written in my book this morning, the number I'd lifted from Ireland's office. I opened my book and read the name, Jonas Meier. I dialed the number and a woman's voice answered.

"Eaton Hotel, how may I direct your call?"

"Yes, may I speak to Jonas Meier please?"

"He's in room 409. One moment while I ring his room."

I waited while the hotel operator made the connection. After a minute or so she came back.

"I'm sorry, there's no answer. May I take a message for Mr. Meier?"

"No, thanks," I said and hung up.

Jonas Meier, a resident of the Eaton Hotel. How did he fit in the picture? A better question might be, did he even fit in the picture? Hell, for that matter, was there even a picture? I'd have to just keep bumbling around in my usual fashion, turning over rocks to see what crawled out. The trouble was I'd have to work fast and get some results before I went to trial. If I didn't have some answers before then, a judge was certain to have me thrown into jail, and my life as a detective would be over.

I made another call, this one to Simon and Simon, attorneys at law. My attorney was Harold Simon. He ran a law firm with his brother Gerald. Formally, they went by Harold and Gerald. Informally, they went by Harry and Gerry. Either way they sounded like a comedy team, but they were each damn fine lawyers. How's that for an oxymoron?

When the receptionist answered I told her my name and asked for Harold. I don't call my attorney often, but she recognized my name and put me through immediately.

"Hello, Pete. How've you been?" Harry said.

"I've been better, Harry," I said.

"No one ever calls an attorney when things are going well," he said. "No one ever calls an attorney and says I'm having a great day, and I just wanted to say hello."

"Quit whining, Harry. If your clients didn't have problems, you and your comedy partner would be out of business."

"Fair enough, Pete. What's up?"

I gave Harry a brief sketch of the case and told him the events of the previous night. He listened without comment, but I knew he was taking notes and thinking.

"The thing is, Harry, I need some time. I don't know what I've got here, but I have to get to the bottom of this. Can you help?"

"Well, there's no question you'll go to trial, Pete, but I'll see what I can do to delay the date. These are pretty serious charges, and the judge will have to give me a reasonable time to prepare a defense. I'll milk that as much as I can. I can't promise how long you'll have, though."

"That's fine, Harry. I'll leave it in your hands. Say 'hi' to Gerry for me."

We said our goodbyes and hung up. I started to leave when the phone rang. I picked it up and said hello.

"This is James Ireland speaking, Mr. Stone. We need to talk."

"As I recall, we did talk, Mr. Ireland, just yesterday as a matter of fact."

"Yes, we did, but that was before you broke into my office. Things have changed now. Gordon Veatch is going to see you put behind bars."

"Maybe or maybe not. Either way, what concern is it of yours?"

"Look, Stone, I don't care one whit about what happens to you, but I know you are trying to help Lucille Hamilton, and I do care about her. Sidney was my best friend, and I am determined to do what I can to help his widow."

"Fair enough, Mr. Ireland. When shall we meet?"

"Now, and it has to be private. If word of this gets to Mr. Veatch, I'll lose my job, and I'll be finished in the aircraft industry."

He gave me the name of a small restaurant east of downtown on Cleveland Street. I was there in ten minutes, and he was waiting at a table near the back wall. He ordered coffee for both of us, and when it arrived he flashed a bill at the waiter who made it disappear. I didn't know what it was about until I tasted my coffee. It was laced with bourbon.

"I hope you don't mind," Ireland said, "but frankly, I need a little courage in my coffee this morning."

"I don't mind. I'm just a little surprised. I didn't take you for a man who drinks early in the day."

"I don't usually," he said, "but these are unusual times. Why in the hell did you break into my office, Stone?"

I shrugged.

"I'm just a bumbling detective, Mr. Ireland, trying to solve a case. You acted pretty cagey when we met yesterday, like you might have something to hide. I wanted to know what it was. I followed you after you left the café and watched you go into the building around the corner. I wondered why. I still wonder why. What do you have to hide, Mr. Ireland? Why do you have an office downtown when you work for an aircraft company on the south side? Why is the best friend of a man recently found dead acting so suspiciously? Those are just a few of the questions I have, and when I don't get answers I go looking for them. It's what I do."

I lit a cigarette and waited for Ireland to respond. He looked toward the door and scanned the restaurant. An early lunch crowd was starting to come in. Ireland leaned forward and lowered his voice.

"Look, Stone, I'm going to lay it on the line for you. I'm working on something important for Stearman Aircraft, something top secret."

He waited for my reaction. I didn't give him one.

"That office you broke into belongs to Stearman Aircraft. It was rented by Mr. Veatch."

"I don't suppose you're going to tell me what you're working on?"

"Not a chance. Like I said, it's top secret."

"Is it common for your company to have an office away from headquarters?"

"It's not uncommon, especially for an important project such as this one. All of the aircraft companies do this. They rent small, nondescript offices in downtown buildings where engineers can work freely without worrying about prying eyes. For all I know, Stearman has other offices just like mine in other parts of town."

"How long have you been working on this project?" I asked.

Ireland stubbed out his cigarette and took a swallow of his alcohol-laced coffee before answering.

"Not long," he said.

A light bulb came on.

"That used to be Hamilton's office, didn't it?" I asked.

Ireland nodded.

"That's right. Sidney was working on this project. When he died, Mr. Veatch asked me to take over. I wish he hadn't. The pressure is tremendous. I'm beginning to understand why Sidney did what he did."

"Look, Ireland, I'm not going away. Why the pressure? Why all the secrecy? What was Sidney Hamilton working on that's causing all the fuss?"

Ireland looked around the room like he expected to be jumped at any minute. I kept my gaze on him and didn't move.

"Look, Mr. Stone. I'm going to tell you something that can't leave this table. If it does, you'll endanger the lives of Lucille and me, not to mention your own."

I continued staring and didn't say a word.

"Sidney was given an assignment, something big. It came down from above."

"From Gordon Veatch?"

Ireland chuckled and shook his head.

"Not from Veatch, from the top, the top brass at Boeing. He was working on it when he... when he... killed himself."

"Wait a minute," I said, "this doesn't make sense. First of all, what was Hamilton working on? Second, why would Boeing come to a Stearman engineer for help? Why wouldn't they use their own engineers? And why would Hamilton kill himself? I thought you guys lived for opportunities like this. I'm not buying that Hamilton was under so much pressure that he killed himself. None of this adds up."

"How do I know why Boeing came to Stearman? This project is top secret. Maybe Boeing wanted to use Stearman to separate their company from the project. Sidney is... was... a great engineer, the best we had. Stearman is a small firm. Hell, we're just a division of Boeing, anyway. By using our engineers instead of their own they probably improved their chances of maintaining security, fewer eyes and all that."

"So what is the project?" I asked. "Why all the secrecy?"

Ireland didn't answer right away. He lit another cigarette and inhaled several puffs. I waited.

"Sidney was working on plans for an advanced bomb sighting device, more sophisticated than anything the military has today. Whoever has this device will have a great advantage in the next war."

"We're not at war," I said.

"No, we're not, but who knows when we will be. It may be in the near future. Things are heating up in Europe. Read the papers. We've got to be ready, and other governments know that. They want what we have, or had."

"Wait a minute. Who wants what we have or had?"

Ireland crushed out his cigarette.

"The Germans are here, in Wichita, snooping around. They know we're on to something."

"Where are the plans now?"

"That's just it. There are no plans. At least we can't find any plans. Sidney is gone, and the plans have disappeared. Veatch is beside himself. All of the brass is. I've been assigned to retrace Sidney's steps, go over his notes, and try to reconstruct the device. The problem is there is precious little to go on. The plans have disappeared like a fart on the prairie."

I didn't think Ireland was telling me everything, but I knew more than I did an hour ago. I suspected that Ireland wasn't half the engineer Hamilton was.

"You say the Germans are here," I said. "Who's here and where are they?"

"I don't know. I'm just repeating what I've heard from Veatch. Apparently he's been contacted. That's all I know."

The waiter arrived with refills. The fresh coffee had bourbon mixed in it, too. A guy could get wobbly-legged drinking Joe in this joint. I thought about Ireland's last remark.

"That doesn't make sense. An important project like this, whatever it is, an engineer might get a shot at only once in a lifetime. If it's as big as you say it is, it would have made Hamilton a big shot, maybe even wealthy. I can't believe he'd cave in to pressure."

"Normally I'd agree," Ireland said, "but there's more to it. It's very involved, and I'm sorry, but I can't discuss it."

"So why did you call me?"

"I told you I'm trying to help. I don't know anything about being a detective, but I do know you're wasting your time breaking into Stearman offices. Mr. Stone, this is top secret stuff. You've already got Mr. Veatch to contend with, and if you're not careful you'll have the United States military on your back. Sidney committed suicide. The best thing you can do for both Lucille and yourself is to accept that. Talk to her, and tell her you talked to me. Whatever you do, stay away from Stearman Aircraft. Mr. Veatch is a very powerful man."

"Yeah, so I've heard," I said.

Ireland nodded at the waiter who brought the bill to the table. He paid it and left a handsome tip.

"Please listen to me, Mr. Stone," he said as he stood up. "It's for your own good."

He put on his hat and left the restaurant. I remained sitting and lit another cigarette. I wanted time to think about what he'd said about this top secret bomb sighting project stuff. I needed time to mull it over, time for it to sink in. Also, my cup wasn't empty. I don't mind leaving coffee on the table, but only a fool walks away from half-finished bourbon.

It was Friday night. I had looked forward to taking Agnes on a date. She'd be feeling low over getting fired, but dinner and dancing would be good for both of us. Over the phone she'd said she'd love to join me. Nothing she said was seductive in itself, but the way she spoke and the huskiness in her voice had given me a tingle in the old BVDs.

The Gage Brewer Band was playing at the Kaliko Kat, and when I suggested going to hear them, Agnes readily agreed. Gage Brewer was local talent, but good. We'd both heard his guitar playing many times and liked his sound. Also, while I looked forward to dinner, dancing, and drinks in the company of Agnes, I had another reason for selecting the Kaliko Kat. That was the dance club that Waldo had mentioned being a hangout for his son, Ralph. I thought I'd check it out for myself.

I picked up Agnes at eight o'clock, and she looked terrific, a real knockout. Brunette curls peeked out from beneath a stylish new hat with a scarlet plume that had probably set Agnes back a week's tips.

"You're looking mighty fancy, sweetheart," I said in my best Bogart imitation.

"Why, thank you, Pete," Agnes said and smiled. "I'm feeling mighty fancy tonight."

She gave me a peck on my cheek when I opened the car door for her, and I felt that tingle again. I casually adjusted my trousers as I walked around to the driver's side. A breeze from the south had started blowing, and the evening had turned a little chilly, so I had the top up on the roadster. I would have enjoyed seeing the open sky, but a closed car was more intimate.

We chitchatted about nothing in particular as I drove south on Broadway. We reached the corner of Broadway and Harry, and I noticed a couple of hookers standing under a streetlamp. I'm sure Agnes noticed them, too, but neither of us made a remark. We crossed over the John Mack Bridge, and I drove a bit further south and pulled up at the Kaliko Kat. The joint was jumping, but I'd called ahead for reservations, so I wasn't worried about getting a table. It's amazing, I thought, that even in tough times, especially during tough times, people manage to find a couple of bucks to get away and forget.

We decided to have drinks before dinner.

"No reason to eat on an empty stomach," I said.

We agreed on martinis, cold, dry, and with olives. I lit cigarettes for both of us while we waited for the drinks to arrive.

"Oh, look," Agnes said. "Gage has a female vocalist with the band tonight."

And he did. The Gage Brewer Band was constantly evolving, adding or dropping a member as gigs and opportunities changed. Tonight, a young, twenty-something redhead who went by the name of Cricket was crooning softly into the microphone in a bluesy-folksy sort of way. The young woman looked stunning in a floor-length green gown. The only jewelry she wore was a single emerald on a gold chain, just enough decoration to add to her beauty without overpowering it.

I looked over at Agnes. She hadn't stopped staring at the singer. She was smiling, but her smile was wistful, and her eyes were moist. Our drinks arrived.

"What shall we drink to?" I asked.

"How about toasting what might have been?" she said.

"I've got a better idea," I said. "Let's drink to what might still be."

Agnes smiled, and our glasses clinked together. The martini was icy and biting. We smoked and drank and enjoyed the music. Cricket was a tiny little thing, but her voice was mellow and full, and her sound was genuine, real. I had little trouble imagining her suffering the sorrows she sang about in her songs. She could belt out a tune.

The club was full, mostly couples or small groups sitting at tables, but I noticed one table in the corner that seemed to have a lot of activity. The light was dim in the corner, but I could see a man in his thirties sitting at the table with a blond bimbo at his side. Nothing unusual there. The man was dressed well, maybe a little too well. His tailor wasn't from Wichita. He wore a well-cut, charcoal-gray pinstripe suit over a dark shirt and a purple tie garnished with a diamond stick pin. He had a diamond ring on his right pinkie finger and another rock on his left ring finger. Even in the dim light, the man sparkled. The bimbo sparkled, too, but I ignored her. Her date ignored her, too. He was preoccupied with the traffic coming to his table.

Every so often a young man dressed in a suit would come by and lean over the table. Mr. Diamond would whisper something in his ear, and the young man would leave. A few minutes later a different young man would come by, and the routine would repeat itself. After watching this for a couple of times, I noticed that each young man would reach under a napkin on the table, retrieve something and slide it into his pocket. I couldn't see what it was, but it didn't take much imagination to assume it was drugs.

The waiter came by our table and hovered at my elbow.

"Agnes, how does a Kansas City strip steak sound?" I asked.

"Delicious."

"How do you want those steaks?" the waiter asked.

"Rare," I replied.

The waiter nodded.

"Make them so rare that if there's a decent vet in the joint, he can revive them," I said.

The waiter nodded and left.

We'd had a couple of martinis while we waited, and I was feeling light on my feet.

"Agnes, darling, may I have the honor of this dance?" I said.

She giggled and rose to her feet.

"I think I feel tipsy," she said.

"Good. If I step on your feet, I can blame you," I said.

She giggled again. The band played a slow number, and we waltzed together. Maybe it was the booze, maybe it was the music, but when Agnes leaned into me our bodies moved as one. I felt that tingle again and had to do an awkward half step to adjust the equipment below the belt. I reddened when Agnes looked up at me, but she just smiled and put her head on my shoulder. We continued to dance. She was a terrific dancer, and I didn't step on her feet.

Dinner was delicious, and the steaks were grilled perfectly. I took a bite and glanced over at the table in the corner. Another young man in a suit approached Mr. Diamond. This young man I recognized. I stopped chewing as Ralph Waldo leaned down and listened, just as the others had done. Ralph slipped his hand under the napkin and stood up with his hand going into his suit pocket, all in one motion. He moved toward the exit and disappeared. Agnes and I finished our meals.

After the waiter cleared the table, we smoked cigarettes and sipped coffee and brandy.

"Pete, can I ask you a question?" Agnes said.

"Sure."

"Are you working on a case tonight or are you on a date with me?"

I must have looked surprised, because I was.

"What do you mean?"

"I mean you've been ogling that table in the corner all evening."

"Agnes, you've got an eye for detail. The answer to your question is I'm on a date with you, a very nice date, I might add. I had hoped I would enjoy your company, and I am, even more than I expected. However, I saw something tonight that disturbed me."

"You mean young Ralph Waldo?" she said.

Again I was surprised.

"You do have an eye for detail," I said. "You know Ralph?"

"Of course I do. I see him occasionally. He drops in at the Broadview to speak to his father from time to time. At least he used to, before today. I've never met him actually, but Waldo talks about his son. I gather there's some friction between the two. Sometimes when we weren't busy I'd stop by Waldo's shoeshine stand to visit or he'd have a cup of coffee in the restaurant even though the boss hated seeing him sitting there. I love what you did with your breakfast this morning, throwing it in his face. Good for you. I wish I could have seen it. I always served Waldo. He's a real gentleman, and I enjoy visiting with him."

"I admire your courage, Agnes, and you're right. Waldo is a gentleman. He also happens to be one of the most intelligent and well-read people I've ever known. But Ralph is a problem, I'm afraid. He's been in trouble before, and I think he's mixing with the wrong element again."

I glanced over at Mr. Diamond's table.

"Agnes, would you mind sitting here alone for just a few minutes? I'd like to speak to that man if you don't mind."

Agnes smiled and nodded.

"Sure. Go ahead, Pete. I'll be fine."

"Agnes, you're a doll," I said, and I meant it.

I signaled the waiter for another round of drinks and rose from the table. Agnes squeezed my hand, and I strolled toward the table. When I got about ten feet away, a big galoot from a nearby table stood up and blocked my path.

"Something I can do for you, Buster?"

I looked up. The man was as wide as a door.

"I've got nothing to say to you, Mac," I said, "out of my way."

I moved forward, and he put a meaty paw on my chest.

"Well I got something to say to you, smart guy," he said. "Nobody sees Mr. Dexter without he says so, see. And Mr. Dexter ain't said so. So go on, get outta here."

He gave me a shove, and I rocked back. I watched Mr. Dexter at his table. He was smiling. So was the bimbo. I could see there was no reasoning with Goliath so I didn't try. I knew I couldn't match his strength, but I also knew he was vulnerable. Every man is. I faked a punch with my right hand, and when he moved to block it, I thrust my left fist into his crotch and grabbed his family jewels. I squeezed them with all I had. He let out a yowl and went to his knees. When he did, I drove my right fist through his nose, and he fell back moaning and rolling on the floor. I stepped around him and approached his boss's table. Dexter's expression hadn't changed. He was still smiling and looking supercilious, like he was Caesar watching gladiators spar in the Coliseum.

"Well done, sir," he said, "well done. No one's every bested Johnny like that before. You are amazing. Who are you, if I may ask?"

"The name is Stone," I said, "Pete Stone."

"Well, Mr. Stone, that was marvelous, just marvelous. Please sit down," he said, gesturing toward a chair. "My name is Reginald Dexter. Most people call me Mr. Dexter, but you may call me Reginald if you prefer. Just don't call me Reggie. No one calls me Reggie. I can't abide being called Reggie, but please, do call me Reginald. Have a seat Mr. Stone."

I continued standing and shook my head.

"No thank you, Reginald. This isn't a social visit."

He nodded and smiled.

"Ah, yes. It must be business you want to discuss. Tell me, Mr. Stone, what do you do for a living? I don't suppose you're looking for a job? I would certainly like to have someone with your talents in my employ. Are you available, Mr. Stone? Or may I call you Pete?"

"Stone will do," I said, "and I've already got a job. I'm a private eye."

Behind me I heard moaning and shuffling as Goliath struggled to get to his feet. I wasn't worried about him, though. Music continued playing, and the patrons who had rubber-necked the scuffle had gone back to their dinners and drinks.

"Oh, I see," he said. "You strike me as a loner, a man who likes working for himself, calling his own shots."

I nodded.

"I do," I said. "I'm as independent as a meadowlark on the prairie."

"I understand," Dexter said. "So you are a private investigator, and you've approached my table to discuss business, and yet you refuse to sit with me. What is it you want from me, Mr. Stone?"

"I want you to fire one of your employees."

Reginald raised an eyebrow.

"One of my employees?" he asked. "Whatever do you mean, Mr. Stone? What a preposterous suggestion. What makes you think you know a thing about me or how I make my living?"

"I've been watching you run your little drugstore all evening, Reginald. You have a string of couriers doing your bidding. That's fine. What you do and how you do it is none of my concern. I'm not here to crusade against peddling dope. I've got enough to do as it is, but I want you to quit doing business with Ralph Waldo. As of this minute, he is no longer in your employ."

"Young Waldo is a good boy," Dexter said. "He's dependable, and he knows his place. I don't wish to lose him. Suppose I refuse your request, Mr. Stone? What then?"

I leaned in closely and grabbed his tie and yanked. My face was inches away from his.

"Then this is what's going to happen," I whispered. "First, I'm going to come for you and your goon over there, and I'm going to go through the both of you like shit through a Christmas goose. Then I'm going to call some friends of mine down at police headquarters, and they are going to sift through the pieces and see if they can't find enough evidence to give you a one-way ticket to Leavenworth. Is that clear?"

I had to admit, Dexter kept his cool. I let go of his tie, and he smoothed it back into place. When he spoke his voice was even and measured.

"You win, Mr. Stone, this round at least. As of now, Ralph Waldo no longer works for me. But I'll warn you, no one talks to me like that and gets away with it, no one. As of now you may consider me an enemy, an enemy not to be trifled with, Mr. Stone. I have friends, friends who are much more formidable than the muscular Johnny over there. Watch your back, private eye."

I stood up and backed away.

"See you around, Reggie," I said and walked back to my table.

Agnes had watched the whole thing, of course, and she stared at me with a saucer-eyed expression when I returned.

"Pete, I've never seen anything like that," she said. "I thought that giant was going to crush you."

"Not today, sweetheart," I said.

"Well, what did you say to that man, and what did he say to you?"

I replayed a short version of our conversation for Agnes, leaving out the part where I had to watch my back. We chatted for a while longer while we finished our coffee and smoked cigarettes, but the dancing mood had left us, and before long I paid the check, and we left.

It was around midnight when we arrived at Agnes's place. We sat in the car for a moment under the moonlight. When we kissed, Agnes squeezed my arm and asked me to come in. We stepped through the door, and I stood behind her and slipped off her wrap. She took off her hat, and I brushed her dark curls aside and lightly kissed the back of her neck.

"Umm, that's nice," she said.

I moved to her ear and nibbled as I unzipped the back of her dress. It fell to the floor, and Agnes stood in her silky dainties. Still standing behind her, I unhooked her brassiere and let it drop. I slid down her panties admiring the curves of her body. She turned around slowly and the view from the front was stunning.

"My god, you're beautiful," I said in a hoarse whisper.

She smiled and leaned into me, and we kissed with hunger and greed. I lifted her into my arms and carried her into the bedroom where we fell onto the bed, and into the wee hours of the morning we held each other and enjoyed each other's pleasures. Afterward, we lay in each other's arms and chatted and cuddled and drifted off to sleep.

It was still dark outside when I opened my eyes. Moonlight shone through the window. I figured I'd been snoozing for a couple of hours. My watch read five o'clock. I looked over at Agnes. Her breathing was slow and steady. I picked up my clothes and went into the bathroom and washed my face. When I came out I was dressed. Agnes rolled over and squinted in the dim light.

"Leaving so soon, Pete? I thought I'd make you breakfast."

"I'll have to take a rain check, sweetheart. I've got to get back on the case."

She smiled and nodded.

"Pete," she whispered. "I had a wonderful evening. It's been a long time."

I leaned over the bed and took her in my arms and gave her a long, slow kiss.

"I had a good time, too, doll, and you were terrific. We should have thought of this a long time ago."

She gave me a squeeze that I returned, and I blew her a kiss as I left. Outside, a hint of pink shone in the eastern sky, but moonlight provided most of the illumination. I whistled softly as I walked to the street to get into my car. Maybe my whistling distracted me. More likely it was the movie reel running through my head, replaying the previous evening's activities. Whatever it was, I didn't hear any footsteps, I didn't hear any movement, and I wasn't aware of a heavy object swinging through the air. At least I wasn't aware until it was too late. By that time the object had landed on the back of my head, and before the sun came up, my lights went out.

When I came to it was still morning, and the neighborhood was quiet. I lay on my back and tried to gather my thoughts. A heavy pressure was on my chest, and for a moment I thought I might be having a heart attack, but my hands groped around and fell on something large, smooth, and cool. It was a rock about the size of a softball or small melon. It weighed several pounds and had served as a perfect blackjack. I lifted it from my chest and tossed it aside.

Who'd whacked me in the head, I wondered? I reached for my wallet and discovered it had been untouched. My money was still in it. I checked for my watch, and it was on my wrist. It read just past six-thirty. Obviously, robbery was not the motive. I looked down at the large stone lying in the street.

Well, Pete, I thought to myself, it looks like someone is still trying to get your attention, this time by knocking out Stone with a stone.

A light came on in Agnes's house. She must have gotten up, but I didn't see any movement and decided not to go back in. I didn't want to worry her. I got in my car and drove away, rubbing the bump on the back of my noggin. Getting conked in the head by a stone was a lousy way to start the day. The guy had to use a stone, but I idly wondered what the mystery man would have done if my last name had been Flowers or Rose or even Cotton. Oh, never mind, I thought.

Saturday, May 1

I stared in the mirror and didn't like what looked back at me. The gash on my head looked meaner than an ex-wife. I was bruised and battered with dried blood caked in my hair. I held a damp cloth to my head and washed away the mess. This was slow going, so I ran a hot shower and stepped in. Ten minutes later I may not have looked as good as new, but I looked as good as I was going to get, and I felt better, too.

I needed coffee and some eggs and didn't feel like making my own, so I put on a clean shirt and suit. With my hat resting lightly on my sore head, I was ready for the day. As I closed the door, I picked up the newspaper on the porch and tucked it under my arm.

I drove south on Waco, and as I neared Douglas, I tried to imagine who was trying to get my attention. Slashed tires and crushed stones in my car. A bonk on the head with a stone. The symbolism was giving me a headache, but who was the culprit? Reginald Dexter could have had one of his goons knock me in the head early this morning, but I hadn't even met Dexter before my tires were slashed.

Gordon Veatch? Possibly. He wanted me off the case, why I didn't know, but I intended to find out. Still, this didn't seem the style for a man in Veatch's position. Guys like that were used to giving orders and being obeyed. When a man didn't obey, someone, an underling, tossed the guy out. Maybe Veatch was behind this. Maybe he'd hired a thug or two to take me out. I glanced at the Broadview as I passed by it and turned east on Douglas. I pulled over at the Eaton Hotel.

The coffee was hot and strong, and the eggs and bacon brought me back to life. I enjoyed it all before leaning back to smoke a cigarette. I caught the eye of the waitress and asked if the hotel manager was in this morning. He was and in a few minutes, he appeared at my table. I asked him to join me, and we visited for several minutes. After our conversation, he left, and I opened the paper.

A guy I didn't know by name, but who I had seen in here often nodded a greeting.

"Any baseball scores?" he asked, indicating the paper.

"Here, help yourself," I said and handed over the sports section.

I opened the paper to the front page and the headline— LOCAL WOMAN MURDERED—screamed at me in bold type. I scanned the story for details and froze when I read the name of the victim. The story went on, giving details that I would only recall later. Suddenly my head began to throb, and my stomach wasn't feeling so good either. I got up and headed for the men's room in the lobby.

I reached the men's room and found a toilet just as my breakfast came up and found the light of day. I stood over the toilet and felt my insides heave. After a few moments I went to the sink and washed up with a cool, damp towel. I held the towel on the back of my neck and breathed deeply. I felt better. Not good, but better.

I knew I wouldn't feel good for some time. I wouldn't feel good until a murder had been solved, probably two murders. Somewhere in Wichita there was a killer. Somewhere in my town a murderer ran loose, and I was determined to find this murderer and bring him to justice. I was going to find the man who had killed a woman who had loved to spend time in her garden, who had loved to tend her flowers, who was too gentle to harm a simple spider. I was going to find out who killed Alice Bennett.

I was in McCormick's office, talking to him about what I'd read less than an hour ago. We each wanted to know what the other one knew, and each of us was reluctant to give away too much.

"What do you know about this, Stone?"

"I don't know a damn thing, but I'm going to find out."

"Is this related to your case?"

"I don't know, but the geography is awfully coincidental. Alice Bennett lived across the street from the Hamiltons, and I don't like coincidences."

"Yeah, I know. I don't either."

I'd called Mrs. Hamilton before going to the police station. I learned that she'd been trying to get a hold of me since last night when I was out with Agnes. She was devastated, of course and wondered if Alice Bennett's murder was related to her husband's death. I wondered the same thing.

McCormick removed the cigar from his mouth and looked me square in the eye.

"Had you spoken to the victim?" he asked. "I mean besides the time you went to her door and asked her to sit with Mrs. Hamilton."

I rubbed the back of my neck and touched the bruise on my head. Mac noticed this, of course, but he didn't ask about it.

"Yeah, I spoke to her on a Saturday. That would have been two weeks ago. I'd just been contacted by Mrs. Hamilton the afternoon before. I was on the way to see Mrs. Hamilton when I noticed Alice Bennett tending her garden. She didn't say much, though. She expressed concern over the disappearance of Mr. Hamilton. She seemed like a nice lady."

I neglected to tell McCormick about Alice Bennett seeing Mr. Hamilton the morning he disappeared. That was privileged information. McCormick looked at me like he knew I wasn't telling him everything. No one ever accused Mac of being stupid.

"What happened to your head, Stone? Someone try to knock some sense into your skull?"

I was beginning to think McCormick didn't care for me.

"I wish I knew," I said. "Somebody blindsided me."

"Robbery?" he asked.

"No. He didn't take anything. Just bopped me on the bean and disappeared into the dark."

I wanted to get back to the murder.

"What have you got, Mac? What do you know?"

The lieutenant grunted.

"It's all in the papers," he said. "Her husband discovered the body when he came home from work last night. She had been working in a garden in the backyard. She died from a blow to the head. Someone used an ordinary rock, probably from her own garden. It was lying next to the body."

I thought about the rock I'd found on my chest this morning.

"Is the husband a suspect?"

McCormick looked at me for a moment before speaking.

"No, no he's not a suspect. He was at work all day. He has a solid alibi with lots of coworkers as witnesses."

"How about the neighbors? Anybody see anything?"

"Stone, I'm not here to serve you steak on a platter. If you want anything else, read the papers and stay out of my way. That's a warning, Stone. You work your case and leave this alone. As far as the police are concerned, your guy committed suicide. If your client wants you to investigate that, that's her business. This case is a murder, and it falls under my jurisdiction. I don't want you mucking up the works. You got that? You start poking around in this, and you'll end up with more than a bruised head."

I held my tongue and nodded. I was angry, and McCormick knew it. He brushed the air with the back of his hand, his usual signal that our conversation was over. As usual, I couldn't keep my mouth shut.

"Just one more thing, Mac. Find the son of a bitch. Find him and put him away and do it fast, because if I ever get my hands on him, there won't be pieces big enough for you to arrest."

McCormick glared at me as I put on my hat and left.

"Oh, Mr. Stone, it's just awful. She was such a dear person, and a dear friend, too. She wouldn't harm a fly. Why did this happen? Who would do such a thing? Why?"

Mrs. Hamilton held her face in her hands and sobbed. I gave her my handkerchief, and she dabbed at her eyes. I'd driven to her place after leaving McCormick's office.

"This is so terrible. First, Sidney is murdered and now Alice. What's happening?"

I didn't remind her that the police still listed Mr. Hamilton's death as a suicide. I had to give it to the gal. Once she made up her mind, nothing would change it. Mrs. Hamilton wasn't alone when I arrived. James Ireland was with her, offering consolation. He looked at her and gave her shoulders a squeeze.

"It's been especially difficult for Lucille, of course."

Mrs. Hamilton patted his hand and stepped away.

"You gentlemen sit down. I'll get some coffee."

I begged off.

"Thank you for the offer, Mrs. Hamilton, but I think I should be going. I'm deeply sorry about Mrs. Bennett's death. I'll let you know when I find anything new."

I shook hands with Ireland, and she led me to the door. I stepped out onto the porch, and she stood in the doorway.

"It looks like I'm the only one who believes my husband was murdered," she said.

"Don't be too hasty," I said. "There are at least two others who believe it. I may not have proof, but I never discount a wife's instinct. I believe your husband was murdered, too."

"Well. Mr. Stone, I'm pleased to hear that you take me seriously. That is comforting. But you said two people believe Sidney was murdered. You're one. Who is the other?"

I put on my hat and stepped off the porch.

"The murderer," I said.

I was in the neighborhood so I decided to stop in at Tom's Inn. I wasn't famished, but a cold beer sounded good. Ten minutes after I left Mrs. Hamilton, I was sitting on a barstool sipping a draft beer.

"Hey, Pete, the way you handled that bruiser the other night was pretty good," he said. "Leonard's not a bad guy, just not too bright, that's all. You ever find out who slashed your tires?"

Tom was wiping the bar with a damp cloth.

"No idea," I said and put my hat on the stool next to me.

Tom stared at my skull and let out a low whistle.

"You look like hell. Did the guy who slashed your tires do that?"

I repeated my first answer.

"No idea."

"No idea, no idea," Tom said. "Someone slashes your tires. Someone conks you on the head, you don't know anything. You have no idea. What makes you think you're a detective?"

"No idea."

Tom shook his head and tipped my empty glass under the stick. He placed it in front of me with a fresh coaster under the glass.

"All kidding aside, Pete, you better be careful. Someone's playing rough."

I nodded and asked him if he'd seen the morning paper. He had.

"Jesus, that was terrible. Right here in our town. Does the Bennett murder have anything to do with your case?"

I told him I didn't know. We discussed the proximity of her murder to the Hamilton home, and I told him the same thing I'd told Mac about not liking coincidences.

"I don't like it, Tom. I don't like it one bit, and I'm angry. Hamilton's death is a shame, but I never met him. I only met Mrs. Bennett once, but I felt like I knew her. She was a simple, kind soul. She didn't deserve to die like that."

"Maybe the cops will come up with a suspect," Tom said.

"They'd better," I said. "They'd better find a suspect before I do. Right now I feel helpless. The cops think Hamilton committed suicide, but Mrs. Hamilton is sure it was murder. I don't have a clue or a suspect, but I believe her, and I'm on her payroll. I hope I'm not giving her false hope. I don't feel like I'm accomplishing much."

Tom put his elbows on the bar and leaned forward.

"You may not feel like you're doing much, Pete, but sometimes doing the right thing, even if it's a little thing, can turn out to be pretty important. Maybe you don't recognize it, and maybe it's not much, but it's important, nevertheless. Sometimes we don't know what's important to another person."

"Yeah, I suppose you're right. I don't know."

"Look, let me tell you a story, a story about a buddy of mine, a story he told me. It happened to him."

I nodded and waited.

"This is the way he tells it. My buddy, his name is Jerry, is walking downtown one day, early in the afternoon it was. He's just finished a sandwich and a beer, and now he's headed back to work. He's got one of those jobs where he uses his back more than his brains, lifts cartons of fruits and vegetables all day. He works in the Wholesale Grocery Warehouse on East William. You know where that is?"

I did and said so.

"Good. So he's walking along, feeling good after his lunch and his beer, and suddenly he hears a couple of loud pops up the street. Gunshots. Someone screams, and then there's a lot of commotion. People start running, and a dark sedan squeals away from the curb and races around the corner."

"What's he do?" I asked.

"Well, see, that's the strange thing. Everybody's running away from the scene, but he runs toward the scene. Why? I don't know. Who knows why? Curiosity? To see if he could help? Who knows? Maybe an angel whispered into his ear, I don't know. But he runs ahead against the crowd, and he sees a man lying on the sidewalk. The guy's been shot, but he's alive. So my buddy, Jerry, crouches down on the sidewalk and cradles the guy's head in his arms and talks to him. You know, soothing stuff to keep him calm. 'You're gonna be all right. Help is on the way. Hang in there.' That kind of thing."

I nodded.

"So the thing is help does arrive. The ambulance gets there, a couple of guys put pressure bandages on the wounds, they load him on a stretcher, and off they go sirens blaring. That's the last my buddy sees of him. The next day he reads in the paper about a shooting downtown, it gives the victim's name which means nothing to my buddy, and it says the guy is expected to recover, which does mean something to my buddy. I mean Jerry didn't know the guy and really didn't help him all that much, but by now he cares about him, you know? And he's happy the guy's going to make it. He mentally wishes him well. Life goes on, and Jerry puts it out of his mind."

"Nice story," I said. "Not a great story but a nice story."

"There's more."

"Good."

"So a few days go by, and like I say, my pal hasn't given the incident another thought. Then one evening he's leaving the warehouse after his shift, ready to go home, and a shiny, black Cadillac pulls up next to him. A guy gets out on the passenger side, big guy, all muscle and asks him to get in the car. Says his boss would like to talk to him. Jerry looks into the car and sees another big guy behind the wheel. They look like the kind of guys who don't hear the word 'no' very often, you know what I mean? He figures he's got no choice. The guy opens the rear door, and Jerry sees another man sitting in back. The man gives him a nod and waves a couple of fingers.

"So Jerry gets in the car, and the guy in the back shakes his hand and introduces himself. Jerry recognizes the last name, and the man says he's the father of the guy who got shot. Jerry wonders how this guy knows him. He doesn't recall mentioning his name at the scene of the shooting, but everything was hectic and crazy. Maybe he did. Anyway, this guy knows him. My buddy looks the man over and realizes he's talking to a big league player. I mean this guy is decked out in the finest threads, silk tie, French cuffs on his sleeves, a beaver skin hat, the works. He's smoking a big cigar, and he offers one to Jerry and gives him a light. It's Cuban, the first one Jerry's ever tasted. He also pours him a drink, right there in the car, and the bourbon is smooth and mellow. It's better than anything you'll find in this city, over or under the table. My pal figures this guy must be connected to the mob or something, but he's smart enough not to ask."

"So what happens?"

"Well, nothing really. They drive west on Douglas. They cross over the river and meander through the park going no place in particular. But while they're driving, the man in back is asking

Jerry questions, personal questions like 'How's your wife? Tell me about your family. How are your parents doing?' Questions like that. And the thing is, my buddy tells me later, this guy listens. I mean he really listens. He doesn't just nod at all the appropriate places trying to be polite. He's really listening to Jerry, like he really cares about him, you know?"

"So that's it, they talk?"

"Yeah, they talk. Jerry says the guy was a terrific conversationalist. You know what a terrific conversationalist is?"

I shook my head.

"That's a guy who keeps his mouth shut and lets you do all the talking. Get it? Well, that's what this guy does. He asks questions, and he listens, and Jerry tells him about his family. He and his wife have a daughter going to Kansas State College, studying to be a nurse. His father is dead, but his mother is alive. She recently fell and broke her hip, that sort of thing. And for the better part of an hour, they ride around, enjoying their cigars, sipping bourbon, and talking about family."

I lit a cigarette and tossed the burnt match into the ashtray.

"After their ride, the car pulls up in front of Jerry's house. Jerry never told the man where he lived, but the man knew, you know? They shake hands, and then the guy does something weird, some sort of European thing, I guess. He takes Jerry's face in his hands, and he kisses him on both cheeks. Jerry's a little stunned by this behavior, but before he can do anything, the man speaks. 'You're a saint,' he says. 'Thank you. Thank you for my son.' The car door opens, and Jerry gets out. The car drives off, and Jerry never sees the man again."

"A little odd, maybe, but nothing extraordinary," I said.

"There's more."

"Ah."

"The next day Jerry walks to work, just like every other day. Except when he returns home, there's a car sitting in the driveway. Jerry's never owned a car, couldn't afford one. Now this car's not a Cadillac, it's a Ford, but it's new, and it's titled to Jerry."

"And Jerry's unknown benefactor paid for it?"

"He doesn't know, but who else could it be? And get this. Jerry and his wife have been scraping their nickels and dimes together to send to Kansas State for their daughter's tuition, and suddenly they get a receipt in the mail from the college. Their daughter's education has been paid in full. Another receipt arrives from Wesley Hospital. His mother's bills have been paid. Overnight my pal is in the black and driving a new car to boot."

"The unknown man must have been pretty grateful."

"Yeah, he must have been grateful. That's my point, Pete. I mean, Jerry has told me a dozen times, he really didn't do anything, you know? He held a guy in his arms until help arrived, that's all. Not much, but that was enough, and that's my point. Maybe you think you haven't done much with this case, maybe you think you aren't doing much now, but maybe you are. Maybe someone is really grateful, and maybe you shouldn't be so hard on yourself. You never know, you know what I mean?"

Agnes gasped.

"Oh, Pete, what happened to you?"

I touched my tender pate.

"Someone outside your door rang my bell," I said.

"Oh my god, are you all right? Did you see who it was? Did he rob you?"

The questions came at me like bullets fired from a Tommy gun. I was in her living room. I'd called her from Tom's Inn and told her I wanted to talk to her. She told me to come right over.

"I'm okay, Agnes. A little bruised is all. I didn't see who it was, but robbery wasn't the motive. I still have my wallet."

"This has to do with the case you're on, doesn't it?"

"Probably, but I can't be sure. Reggie Dexter took offense over our conversation. I can't rule him out. He's the kind who plays for keeps, and he always has someone warming up in the bullpen to do his dirty work."

"I didn't like his looks either," Agnes said, "and I didn't like the way he was using Ralph."

"Neither did I. What I did like was the way you handled yourself, the way you noticed things and made the correct assumptions. I think you have a gift for this business, Agnes. How would you like to work for me, be my assistant?"

"Oh, Pete, really? Do you really think I could help you or would I just be in the way? I couldn't stand it if this were just a handout."

"Don't worry, doll," I said. "This isn't a handout. I could use your help."

"And I could use a job."

We stared at each other.

"I guess if I do this," she said, "we'd have to give up the lovemaking."

I nodded.

"It wouldn't work any other way," I said.

"I knew you'd say that," she said, "and you're right. Well, the lovemaking is great, but a girl's got to eat. I'll take the job, Pete."

I smiled and nodded.

"And I knew you'd say that," I said.

We shook on it, and I had an assistant.

"So when do I start?" she asked. "What's my first assignment? Am I going to be your secretary?"

"Not a chance, kiddo. I need an assistant, not just someone to answer the phone. I'm throwing you to the wolves. Let's see how you do."

I laid out her first assignment, and she listened carefully and didn't flinch. Frankly, I didn't know what role Agnes would play as my assistant, but I knew she'd be an asset, and I was glad to have her on board.

I drove to my office to make a quick call to Ellis Waldo. I found him at home, we chatted briefly, and I told him getting fired was a raw deal. In his philosophical fashion he didn't seem bitter. We chatted some more, I made a suggestion or two, and he seemed appreciative. He thanked me, and I hung up.

Back on the street, I drove east on Douglas. I had to swerve out of the way of a streetcar, and I bounced over the brick street. I turned north on Hillside and drove past the college. I turned east again on Twenty-First, and when I got to Oliver I pulled up in front of a store with a sign over the door that read "Doc's Clocks."

When I entered the store, a dinging bell announced my arrival. A small gray-haired man was standing behind the counter looking through a jeweler's loupe at the innards of a watch. He set the loupe on the counter, put on a pair of gold, wire-rimmed glasses, and looked up at me.

"Pete Stone, it's good to see you," he said, waving his arms. "Come in, come in."

"How are you, Doc? It's good to see you, too," I said.

"What brings you in, Pete? A social call or are you looking for a new timepiece?"

"I'm not sure, Doc. Maybe a little of each," I said.

Doc and I had done business with each other on several occasions. Over the years, I'd purchased a number of clocks and watches, some for gifts, and some because I liked having them around. Doc knew more about timepieces than any person I'd ever met.

"Say, Doc, I saw a clock the other day I really admired, a Chelsea Brass Marine. You wouldn't happen to have one would you?"

"That's a nice clock, Pete. Was it in good condition?"

"Yes, it was. It was polished and mounted on a mahogany base. It looked beautiful," I said.

Doc stroked his chin.

"Well, I don't have one in the store, but I'm sure I could order one if you'd like," he said.

"That's okay, Doc. I'll let you know if I change my mind. What else have you got that I might be interested in?"

We chatted for the better part of an hour, and Doc showed me several nice clocks he had recently taken in. I finally settled on a Seth Thomas Banjo clock that would fit perfectly in my office. Now that Agnes was coming with me I might as well dress up the place. I settled up with Doc, and we shook hands and said our goodbyes.

I needed to think, and when I need to think, I like to drive. I dropped the top on the Jones Roadster and headed west out of town. There was a breeze from the south, the sun was warm, and the country roads were dry and dusty. I drove past patchy fields of green, winter wheat swaying in the breeze, still a couple of months shy of ripening for harvest. The Kansas countryside is noted for its golden waves of grain, but I've always been partial to the sight of late April and early May wheat when it's still green, young, and fresh.

Farmhouses painted white or peeling to gray stood near the road every mile or so. Here and there a farm wife waved from a sagging wooden porch. Mangy dogs chased the car and barked at the tires. I nodded and waved at a Bible salesman driving in the opposite direction. From what I gathered, Bible sales were fairly brisk in this part of the country. Given the dusty drought, poor crops, and feelings of helplessness, many a farmer turned to the Good Book for signs of hope and understanding, and opportunistic salesmen appeared to fill the need. Some of them were honest, many of them were scam artists, and all seemed to be making a living.

I thought about what I had so far. Sidney Hamilton was dead. The police ruled it a suicide, but his widow swore he'd been murdered. One of them was right, and my money was on Mrs. Hamilton. Sidney Hamilton had been working on a top secret project for Stearman, and according to his best friend, James Ireland, he was under a lot of pressure. For whatever reasons, Gordon Veatch at Stearman wanted me to stay off the case, and before long I'd be dragged into court and forced out of the business for good.

Someone killed Alice Bennett, and although I couldn't prove a connection to Hamilton's death, I didn't like the fact that they were neighbors. That was too big a coincidence. Someone had slit my tires outside of Tom's Inn and had left stones on my car seat. Someone (the same someone?) had conked me on the head with a rock outside of Agnes's home. Reginald Dexter had said I'd made him an enemy, but I hadn't crossed paths with Dexter until after that evening at Tom's when my tires were slashed. I had a name, Jonas Meier, I found on a note pad in Ireland's office, but I didn't know Meier or have anything on him.

And then there was that clock, the Chelsea Brass Marine, with that cryptic Shakespeare quotation, "Time is the justice that examines all offenders." I couldn't shake that clock and that quotation. I drove on and mulled over the facts.

Every few miles I'd turn right and then left again so I was headed in a northwest direction. I drove through Andale and Mt. Hope without stopping and passed the Haven Cemetery. When I came to the correction line, I drove another half mile west and pulled in at the farmstead. Hedge apple trees growing in the ditch arched their limbs over the rutted driveway. Hedge apples lay scattered in the driveway, and my roadster bounced as it crushed the gnarly green fruit beneath its tires. An adolescent girl standing in ankle-deep grass waved from the yard and ran into the house.

A shaggy-haired dog, a collie mix, eyed me from a shady spot beneath a small maple near the house. I parked the car at the edge of the grass and kept my eye on the dog. Like an old cow in a pasture, the dog lifted its rear haunches in the air, extended its front legs, and pushed up, coming to all fours slowly. The dog hobbled across the grass toward me and stopped about ten feet short of my car. It raised its head, and with tired effort, offered a single "Woof." Having fulfilled its duty as protector of the castle, the old dog turned and hobbled back to rest in the shade.

From an open window, I heard a woman at a piano singing "The Old Rugged Cross." After a moment, the music stopped, and a screen door on the porch opened. A short, stout woman with hair tied in a bun came through the door and waved "hello." The girl smiled, and the screen door slammed behind them.

"How do, Mona," I said and nodded to the girl.

"Orville's down to the barn," she said. "What brings you out this way?"

"Just needed to get out of the city for a spell," I said. "How's Orville doing?"

Mona went silent and looked down.

"Oh, 'bout the same, I guess."

Orville was a hard worker, scratching at a forty acre patch of dirt, trying to make a living like so many others, but he'd turned bitter these past few years. It began when oil was discovered in this corner of the county, and a horde of men in suits and ties descended on the rural communities waving legal papers and promising riches beyond belief. When Orville read the documents that he couldn't understand, he rubbed his chin and muttered, "I don't know." He must have muttered once too often, because before he knew it, the men in suits had gone across the road to visit Orville's brother, Yancey, who was only too eager to sign. That was three years ago, and today wells were drilling on Yancey's property, undoubtedly drawing oil from a pool that ran beneath Orville's small stake, too. It was more than Orville could stand, and he hadn't spoken to his brother since.

"Here he comes now," Mona said.

We all looked in the direction of the barn as a wiry figure in bib overalls came toward us. He looked like he'd lost some weight.

"Is he alright?" I said. "He isn't sick is he?"

Mona read my concern.

"He's sick, I guess," she said.

"Mona, he isn't dying is he?"

She shook her head.

"No, he isn't dying. He's just quit living."

Another dog, this one a lively, brown, short-haired mutt, raced from Orville's side and jumped up on my leg eager for a scratch and attention. Mona yelled at the mutt to get down, but I patted the pup on the head.

"What brings you out this way?" Orville said, extending his bony hand. I shook it.

"Well you're not going to believe it," I said, "but they plumb ran out of iced tea in Wichita. The only place I could think of that might have some was right here at the forty."

Mona laughed and asked me in, but the shade on the east side of the house was inviting so we took seats in white wicker chairs on the porch. I looked past Orville to the empty rabbit hutches leaning against the side of the barn, another testimony to easy riches gone awry. The hutches had lost their paint and weathered to a dull gray. Tall grass had grown up around the cages, and a couple of the wired doors were hanging open, a pathetic picture of dreams let loose.

Orville believed that a handshake and his word were worth something, and he made the not uncommon mistake of assuming that other men felt the same. So when J.S. Porter, salesman and scam artist, came through the area six years ago promising hope and riches to those who would listen, Orville listened. Orville didn't particularly need riches, but like so many in recent years, he was running low on hope.

Porter, who went by the moniker of "Rajah," was the proprietor of Rajah Rabbitry, a commercial enterprise that began in Wichita. A glib, dapper gentleman, he held his audience spellbound, painting verbal images of the vast amounts of money to be made by breeding and harvesting rabbits. He convinced his "investors" that rabbit pelts were widely valued back east for ladies' coats and gentlemen's hats. He would buy the pelts from all the offspring investors would raise. Furthermore, the rabbits would offer savory meat that would yield a delicious stew for the family table right here in Kansas. And it was so easy. Farmers were already raising pigs and chickens and cattle and such. Raising rabbits would be even easier since, as everyone knew, they were prolific breeders. Why the farmer would be overrun with valuable livestock in only a few months.

Orville listened, and it made sense, so he emptied his savings account and took out a small loan to purchase three females and a male for the princely sum of one hundred dollars. He bought lumber and wire and built several hutches in a couple of days. He bought extra lumber and wire so he could add hutches as the rabbits grew in numbers.

At first, everything went well, and the number of rabbits increased. When the numbers became too large for his hutches, Orville slaughtered and skinned several, keeping the meat for his family. He loaded the pelts into his rusty Ford pickup and went to

Wichita to sell his pelts only to discover that J. S. Porter was gone. He was on the lam, and no one knew where to find him. Rajah Rabbitry was in receivership, and Porter disappeared along with thousands of dollars from hundreds of bilked investors.

Orville continued raising rabbits for a while until his family and neighbors grew tired of rabbit stew. With no market for pelts, the skins were burned in trash fires. After about a year, a virus struck the remaining stock, and within a few weeks all of them were dead, along with Orville's dream of vast riches. Only the overgrown, faded hutches remained.

The screen door slammed behind Mona as she came out of the kitchen with iced tea poured into canning jars. The jars sweated in the heat and water dripped on our chins. I drank my tea unsweetened, but Orville had a fondness for sugar and scooped several teaspoonfuls into his.

Orville asked me how my "detecting work" was going, and I told him I was working on a case, but I needed to get away from the city and think for a while. He and Mona nodded in an understanding way. Neither understood why anybody would ever want to go to town at all except for a rare trip for a bolt of cloth or a new scythe or fuel for the lanterns and such.

"Do you miss the dairy business?" Mona asked.

I raised my empty glass for her to fill.

"I miss this," I said. "I miss the country and the people in it."

Orville and Mona Nicklaus raised their family on forty acres of farmland in a corner of Reno County known as red jaw country. Like other farmers, they fought the weather and the bugs and drought and the fickle prices of wheat and corn and swore a farmer's life was the hardest life there was and complained only a fool would choose such a life, but neither of them would dream of exchanging their lives for any other.

The kids were grown and married and gone except for the youngest girl, Darlene. She was a shy, pretty girl who was still in high school, and she sat on the porch step and listened quietly while the elders chatted. My younger son, Jackie, had spent some time with her before he went into the Navy, and at an appropriate pause in the conversation, Darlene asked after Jackie. I told her last I'd heard he was fine and in Philadelphia, but he expected his ship would be leaving on a cruise anytime. I didn't know when he'd be home again.

Our glasses were empty, and Orville was itching to get the chores done and asked if I'd like to drop a line in the creek before I headed back. I said I surely would, and Orville cautioned me to watch out for the bull. He had several cane poles leaning in the corner of the shed, and I chose one that would work just fine from the creek bank. I rooted around in his garden until I came up with a few worms and dropped them in an empty can. I waved to the family and walked behind the barn and through the orchard and crossed a small pasture until I came to a shady spot along the creek that looked promising. I baited the hook and dropped it into the hole, letting it rest on the bottom where the catfish feed and leaned back against a hedge apple tree.

I got to thinking about the old days, the days that were no longer and maybe never were at all. Getting lost in reverie is a risky pastime best left to solitude and quiet afternoons spent under shady trees. I took a flask out of my pocket and savored the bourbon burning down my throat. I don't doubt my memories, they are crystal clear, but I do doubt their accuracy, more and more as time goes by.

In days gone by, my once-wife Marcie and I would drink tea on the porch on a day like today and watch the kids playing in the yard. We'd pretend our lives would stay the same and never change. It seemed safer that way. Of course, nothing does stay the same.

Each of our children was special, like each other in many ways and totally different in others. Dan was studious and academic by nature, drawn to books and learning, always looking to the future and itching to get someplace else. He was a talented vocalist and earned money singing at weddings and funerals. Before he finished grade school it became obvious that Kansas could not contain his curiosity, and by the time he finished high school, he'd firmed up plans and secured the necessary scholarships to attend college. Ironically, this forward-thinking young man found his niche by studying the past and was now studying history and working as a librarian at a university in Oregon.

Mary Jane had finished high school and married a wealthy farmer who owned land not far from here. Her husband, Gregory Smoot, was not a likable man, and I only saw my daughter when she came to see me. I rarely spoke to her husband.

It was after Jackie left home that our lives really changed. Jackie was impatient. He left high school when he was a senior anxious to join the Navy and see the world. Now he was stationed aboard a destroyer in a shipyard, helping fit the ship for its maiden voyage into the Atlantic. He was a quartermaster petty officer and would be responsible for the ship's navigation, maintaining and reading nautical charts.

Marcie and I saw Jackie off at the train station, and even though we hadn't discussed it, we knew our marriage was over. I don't know exactly when I knew, but I knew. It may have been the long silences, the rolling away from each other in bed at night, the damp handkerchiefs left on the sheets each morning. I no longer owned the dairy delivery business and frankly didn't know where our next check was coming from. Jackie's train chugged over the eastern horizon, and we looked at each other for the first time in a long time, and for the last time. We didn't say much, but we hugged each other. Marcie returned to the house, and I spent the night at the YMCA. A few days later she was gone, and the house was closed up. I never went back.

The daylight was fading, so I drove back to my office where Agnes was waiting to fill me in on what she had learned on her first assignment. We decided to walk down to the Eaton Hotel and discuss it over dinner.

"What'd you find out?" I asked.

"Jonas Meier is German, all right," Agnes said, "and I think he's in Wichita to meet with aircraft manufacturers. I found these phone numbers in his room."

She handed me a crumpled piece of paper with numbers written on it. The numbers were written with the backward slant common to a left-handed writer. Each number had a line drawn through it.

"In his room!" I said. "What if you'd have gotten caught? Jesus, the cops would've thrown the book at you and me, too, Agnes. I told you to watch the guy, not break into his room. "

"Actually, you told me to see what I could find out about the guy," Agnes corrected me, and she was right. That is what I had said. "Besides, I didn't break into his room."

"Then how did you get in?" I asked.

Agnes smiled and nibbled a bite of salad. Several tables were occupied, so I tried to speak quietly. The dining room looked out into the lobby, and across the lobby was a shoeshine stand. Ellis Waldo was popping his rag over someone's shoes. Agnes noticed my gaze. She put her hand over mine.

"What you did for Waldo was nice, Pete," she said, "really nice. He told me how grateful he is."

I feigned surprise.

"Grateful? To me? Why?"

"Don't tell me you had nothing to do with his getting hired, Pete Stone. I don't know how you did it, but I know you pulled some strings. It was a nice thing to do."

I shrugged.

"Waldo's a good guy. He deserves an even break. Back to the question at hand. How did you break into Meier's room?"

"I told you I didn't break in," she said. "I just walked in, posing as the maid."

I raised my eyebrows.

"Not bad, Agnes. How did you work that out?"

She took out a cigarette, and I lit it and one for myself.

"I'd like to tell you I was really sneaky and crafty, but all I did was slip a buck to the regular maid and ask her to get lost for a few minutes. She gave me her cleaning equipment, let me in the room, and disappeared for a quarter of an hour. I went through his clothes, looked under the mattress, and checked the closet and the desk. I found nothing. Then I looked in the trash and came up with that list of numbers. I should have looked there first. I spoke to the maid, and she said she'd greeted him on more than one occasion. She told me he spoke broken English with an accent."

"Nice work, Agnes," I said. "I knew you had detecting skills."

I scanned the list, and one of the numbers looked familiar. I checked my book and found it there, too. It was the number of Gordon Veatch's office.

"Pete, I found something else."

"Go ahead, Agnes. What did you find?"

"It was hidden in the closet on the floor behind a pair of boots."

"And?"

"It was a gun. I'm not sure what kind."

She described the pistol to me.

"It sounds like a Luger," I said. "That makes sense. He must have brought it with him into the country. Did you find anything else?"

"Just the ordinary stuff, clothes, shoes, shaving kit. One other thing was kind of odd, though."

"Yes?"

"He has strange tastes in literature. I saw a book on the nightstand. It was written in German so I couldn't read it, but the cover was very strange, illustrations of weird objects and symbols, like a book on paranormal activity, perhaps."

I thought about that for a moment. Rumors had been circulating about Hitler having a fascination with other-worldly activity. Who knew what was true concerning Hitler? He seemed to be driven by a passionate madness. Maybe Jonas Meier aspired to be like his leader. Maybe Meier was mad, too.

"I agree," I said. "That seems strange, but maybe he's just an odd duck interested in strange phenomena. I'm trying to figure out why an aircraft executive would need to carry a gun."

"Maybe he's the nervous, high strung type," Agnes said.

"Or maybe he isn't just an aircraft executive," I said.

It was getting late, so Agnes left with a wave. I walked back to the office to take care of a few details and locked the door. I thought about going out for a drink, but the country air had left me feeling drowsy, so I decided to drive home.

When I got to my place on Lewellen something caught my eye. A light shone from the kitchen. A car I didn't recognize was parked on the street in front of the house. I drove past my place and parked in the next block. I got out of my car and walked back. I took my gun out of my shoulder holster and held it close to my hip, pointed down.

It was a quiet evening and most people had their windows open. I heard the low rumblings of radio programs and the rustle of pots and pans coming from neighbors' homes. I live on the second floor of a frame house one door from the corner. A wooden stairway runs up the outside wall of the house to my place. I approached the steps cautiously and strained to hear noises from above. I heard nothing, but the windows were closed as I had left them. Only the light suggested the rooms were occupied.

I scaled the steps carefully, trying to avoid making noise, but creaks from the stairs were audible. I neared the top landing and heard muffled voices behind the door coming from the kitchen. It sounded like two men. The curtains were drawn, and I couldn't see inside.

I weighed my options. I could go back down and wait for them to leave and accost them then, which was certainly the safest option. Or I could barge in with my gun drawn and surprise them, and myself, since I had no idea who they were or what they wanted. I didn't want to wait.

I put my hand on the doorknob and turned it slightly. It was unlocked. I took a deep breath, threw open the door, and leaped in with my gun at the ready.

"Hold it right there!" I said. "Put your hands in the air!"

The two men were sitting at the table and fell back in surprise.

"Jesus, Dad, take it easy!" one of them yelled, and I stared into the eyes of my son, Dan. "It's me!"

For a long second or two, nobody spoke. Then the tension fell away, and I crossed the room and hugged my son. The other guy stared with round eyes, and we all started talking at once.

"You scared me to death."

"I didn't know who you were."

"Do you always come into a room like that?"

"Do you always break into a guy's house?"

"You gave me a key, remember?"

Then we were laughing and hugging, and Dan introduced me to his friend.

"Dad, this is Clem Lucas, my friend and colleague."

We shook hands, Clem's eyes still round and staring.

"Is this a typical greeting?" he said.

I laughed and shook my head and assured him this was very unusual. Dan, ever perceptive, cut to the chase.

"You're working on a case, aren't you, Dad? Are you in danger? And please don't try to con me with well-intentioned lies. I want to know if you're in danger."

So I filled him in with no lies, beginning with the discovered body and my hunt for a murderer who may or may not exist. I told him about my new assistant and her detecting abilities. Of course, I failed to mention the crack on the head, the night in jail, the probability that I would soon be arrested, and several other juicy details. I didn't lie, I just didn't tell the whole truth. Dan wasn't fooled in the least, but he knew better than to pursue it. We changed the topic.

"What brings you to Wichita?" I said.

"You," Dan said. "We're on our way to a library convention in Kansas City. The train stopped here, and we decided to get off and say hello. We have to be in Kansas City tomorrow. We'll catch another train in the morning."

"Would you like to stay here?" I asked, knowing the answer would be no. I have a guest room—with one bed—and they were welcome to use it. I knew Dan and Clem would only need one bed. Dan knew that I knew that. But we had a tacit agreement not to discuss it. Dan knew I loved him, and I felt his lifestyle was his business.

"No, thanks, Dad. We've already booked a room downtown."

"Are you sure, Dan? You know you are always welcome here."

"I know, Dad, but we'll be fine."

"So what's the convention about?"

"Microfilm," Dan said, and for the next hour over tumblers of bourbon, Dan and his friend enlightened me on the advances in microfilm. Although it had been invented nearly a hundred years ago, the American Library Association had only sanctioned its use last year, and this convention was intended to educate librarians on its possibilities.

It got late, and I fried some bacon and eggs while the other two made toast and coffee. Dan told me a story about a trip he'd made earlier to Hong Kong.

"It was a gift I gave to myself," he said. "I'd just completed my doctoral thesis, *The United Kingdom of Great Britain and Ireland, An Annotated Bibliography of Documentary Sources*. I worked on the thesis for two years, and I needed a break. I've always been fascinated by the Orient, and I thought why not? It was the greatest experience of my life.

"You know, Dad, there comes a time in a man's life when he receives an understanding, an insight, when he knows that his life will never be any better than it is right at that moment. That moment came to me last summer, Dad. Clem and I had flown to Hong Kong to attend a conference, and we stayed over for a few days to relax and enjoy the culture. Anonymity is a great thing, Dad. No one knew us, and no one cared about us. One evening we were sitting in a bar, actually on an outdoor porch attached to the bar, overlooking the harbor. Red, white, and blue lights reflected off the water. An occasional sampan would drift by. We had just finished a marvelous dinner of roast goose and mango pudding, and I was sipping a glass of French cognac. A small combo played nearby, and couples were dancing. I looked out over the harbor and breathed in the salt air, and I suddenly realized, that right there, right then, was the best moment of my life, and it would never get any better than that. No matter what happens in the future, Dad, I'll always have that moment."

Dan smiled when he finished his story. His friend, Clem, nodded. We chatted into the evening, and when they grew tired, they said their goodbyes and drove off in the unfamiliar car that was parked at the curb. It was probably borrowed from a friend downtown.

That night, I thought of Dan, and thinking of him brought my friend Waldo to mind. They were two of the most intelligent men I knew, yet each was forced to navigate the shoals of society from the fringes, one due to the color of his skin and the other due to a lifestyle frowned on by people who insisted we all live by the same set of rules. I silently cursed the ways of the world.

I wasn't sleepy anymore, so I took a book off the shelf and poured another glass of bourbon. The book was *Modern American Poetry and Modern British Poetry,* edited by Louis Untermeyer. It was a gift from Dan. I turned to page seventy-four and read Walt Whitman's "O Captain! My Captain!" like I often do when I open this volume. I thought of Sidney Hamilton's untimely death as I read the words "... our fearful trip is done,/The ship has weather'd every rack, the prize we sought is won," and pondered his own fearful, fateful trip.

I read a bit of Dickinson and Frost and noticed the hour was approaching midnight. I returned to Whitman and randomly read from "Song of Myself." At the stroke of the hour, the many clocks I owned began their chiming. I closed my eyes and enjoyed the dozen bongs and tinkles and bells from each clock. When I began reading again, I happened upon a line in the forty-fourth stanza that read, "The clock indicates the moment – but what does eternity indicate?" With that line resting in my mind, I turned out the lights and went to bed.

Monday, May 3

On Monday I got a call from my attorney, Harold Simon.

"What's up, Harry? Give me some good news."

"I wish I could, Pete. Gordon Veatch is being a hard ass. I don't know what was in the office you broke into, but it must have been pretty important. He's really screaming the high notes. Claims that you are a threat to national security, a spy for the Germans, ought to be locked up and the key thrown away… you get the picture. According to the complaint his lawyer filed, you're guilty of everything except kidnapping the Lindbergh baby. You didn't, did you?"

"Didn't what?"

"Kidnap the Lindbergh baby."

"Thanks, Harry. You're supposed to be on my side. What was that other thing Veatch said?"

"A threat to national security?"

"No, no, the German spy thing."

"Yeah, right. Veatch claims you are a German spy. I'm looking at a copy of the complaint his lawyer filed with the court."

I pondered that for a moment. Harry broke the silence.

"You still there, Pete?"

"Yeah, yeah. I'm just trying to figure out why Veatch would make that claim. I mean, I broke into his office. He's got me dead to rights there, but why the German spy claim?"

"Beats me," Harry said, and then he went silent for a moment. Finally, he spoke.

"There's more, Pete."

"Let me have it, Harry."

"The judge is impressed with Veatch's complaint," Harry said, "the national security angle and all. He feels it's important to our country's safety to move quickly on this. He wants us in court for a preliminary hearing next Monday. Now, we'll plead not guilty, Pete, and the judge will give me time to prepare a case."

"That sounds routine, Harry. What's the problem?" I heard a sigh on the other end of the line.

"Pete, in light of these charges, I expect the judge to order you taken into custody at the preliminary hearing."

"Damn," I said.

"Yeah, damn," Harry said. "Actually the judge wanted you picked up right away, but I convinced him you aren't a flight risk and you'd show on Monday. He's a friend of mine, and he cut me some slack. I don't know how your case is going, but if you're going to solve it, you'd better move fast. You've got one week, Pete."

One week. I had one week to solve this case. I was convinced along with his widow that Hamilton was murdered, but we were the only two who believed it. There was no doubt that Alice Bennett was murdered, and I was convinced the two murders were connected, but how? What was the connection? Hamilton's murder was surely tied to his work, most likely a top secret project at Stearman. Was he working with the Germans? For the Germans? Against the Germans? Were the Germans even involved? Either way, how did Alice Bennett fit into this? She was just an ordinary housewife who liked to garden in her spare time. Why did she have to die?

No matter what the consequences, I decided I wouldn't quit until I uncovered the culprit or culprits responsible for causing this grief. I'd have an answer within a week, and if I didn't, I'd turn into a fugitive rather than give myself up to the law. I would be no good to anyone locked up, and I wasn't thrilled with the prospect of whiling away behind bars anyway. If I didn't have answers by next Monday, I'd go into hiding. I couldn't tell my lawyer this, because, of course, he would advise against it, reminding me that what I was considering was illegal. I didn't care. Given the choice between doing what's legal and what's right, I've always opted for doing what's right. One thing I've learned is that what is legal and what is right aren't always the same things.

I sat at my desk and lit a cigarette and contemplated my next move. I blew smoke rings and watched them float toward the ceiling. Agnes walked in just as I crushed out my cigarette. She was carrying a potted geranium. I wasn't surprised. Although she'd been my assistant for only a couple of days, she'd added little bits and pieces to my office to make it more attractive. A small painting of a young boy alongside a brook holding a cane pole between his toes hung on one wall near the clock I'd recently purchased. A few magazines lay on a small table that had appeared sometime in the last day or so. I'd had a desk delivered for Agnes, and she set the plant on it.

"Let's go to lunch," I said.

She glanced at the clock. It was a little early for lunch, but what the hell.

"Okay," she said, "something fancy?"

"You bet."

We got in the roadster and drove to Broadway and Main. I pulled up in front of White Castle Hamburgers. There were more White Castle joints around now, but this was the original built in

1921. They succeeded because they made a great hamburger, and who doesn't like a great hamburger? Theirs were small and juicy. They used only the finest meat, and they didn't skimp on the onions. My mouth was watering before I stopped the car.

I parked next to a red and white Swift & Co. truck whose driver was delivering meat and dairy products. The store was open, but we arrived ahead of the regular lunch crowd. There were only a few tables inside, and they were empty. We took one in the back, and I ordered a platter of burgers and two cups of coffee. We inhaled the smell of frying onions and listened to the sizzling grill behind the counter.

Agnes looked around. The place had ambience if your tastes ran to chintzy décor, pungent odors, and good food.

"Talk about fancy," Agnes said. "You really know how to spoil a girl."

"Nothing but the best, my dear, nothing but the best."

I lit cigarettes for each of us while we waited for our food to arrive.

"Agnes, I got a call from my attorney this morning," I said. "We've got one week to solve this case or I'm going to be locked away."

I filled her in on the details. We finished our cigarettes, and our food arrived along with refills of coffee.

"So what's our next move?" Agnes said.

I finished a burger and reached for another.

"We've got to find out who this Jonas Meier is and what he's doing in Wichita," I said.

Agnes nodded and wiped the corner of her mouth with a paper napkin.

"Fair enough," she said. "That makes sense. We know where he's staying. How are we going to handle it?"

I didn't answer right away. I chewed slowly and thought.

"Wait a minute, Pete," Agnes said. "I don't like that look. Don't tell me you don't want me to be a part of this. I'm your partner, remember?"

I raised my eyebrows.

"Partner? Two days ago you were my assistant."

"So I just gave myself a promotion," Agnes said. "Who cares? Assistant, partner, whatever, I'm with you on this."

"Agnes, we know he has a gun. We don't know much else. Until we do, I can't put you in harm's way. If anything happened to you, I couldn't live with myself."

"What about something happening to you? How am I supposed to live with myself if anything happens to you? I can't just sit on the sidelines and wait for the phone to ring. I can't do that. I can't, and I won't."

I leaned back in my chair and smiled.

"Say, you're a real tough cookie aren't you, sweetheart?"

"You bet your ass, buster. Don't get me started. So what are we going to do? Play it cagey or come at him hard and fast?"

"Easy, doll. Let's finish the burgers and think about our next move."

And that's what we did.

When we got back to the office, there was a message from my answering service: call Lucille Hamilton. She answered on the second ring.

"Oh, Mr. Stone, something awful has happened. Someone broke into my home. The place is a mess!"

"Is the house empty now?" I said. "Are you sure there is no one there now?"

"Yes, yes, I looked in every room. I should have called the police, but I think this has something to do with Sidney's death.

His study is a mess. Everything is all over the floor. Should I call the police?"

I advised her to wait until I arrived before getting the police involved. I gave Agnes some instructions and headed for the Hamilton home. It took seven minutes to travel west on Douglas and reach her home.

Mrs. Hamilton was right. The place was a mess. Books had been thrown from the shelves, pictures taken off the walls, cushions lifted from the couch and chairs, but the real damage was in Hamilton's study. Desk drawers had been emptied and turned upside down. A file cabinet had been rifled, its contents spilled onto the floor. Papers, pencils, pens, slide rules, drafting equipment, and office supplies were everywhere. Someone had hit the room hard.

I looked at my watch. It was just after 1:00 PM.

"When did you discover this?" I said.

"About half an hour ago. I called and left a message for you. I've been frantic. Who did this? What do they want? What was Sidney involved in?"

All good questions, but I didn't have the answers, yet. I walked through the kitchen to the back door. The backyard was surrounded by shrubs that shielded the neighbors' view of the door. I checked the lock and found scratches that could have been left by a lock picker. The burglar probably picked the lock and was inside the house in less than two minutes.

"You discovered this a half hour ago. Where were you this morning?"

"At the market. I always go to the market on Monday morning. I used to walk and have the groceries delivered."

She paused and dabbed at her eyes with a handkerchief.

"Now, I have the car, so this morning I drove. I was only gone for about an hour."

An hour. Plenty of time for a burglar to break in and take the place apart, but only if the burglar was watching and waiting for her to leave, or perhaps the burglar knew her habits. Someone could have watched her leave and taken a chance she'd be gone for a while. What would have happened if she'd returned home sooner? What would the burglar have done if she had returned while he was still in the house? I shuddered.

"Who did this, Mr. Stone?"

"I don't know, but I intend to find out. Whoever it was probably was looking for the plans your husband was working on. From the looks of the place, he didn't find them. If he had, not everything would be a mess. This looks more like he looked everywhere and left empty-handed."

She dabbed her eyes again.

"Do you think he'll be back?"

"I don't think so. He didn't find what he wanted here, so he'll have to look someplace else. I don't think you have to worry about his returning. I'll check with the neighbors before I leave to see if anyone saw anything."

"Thank you, Mr. Stone." She looked at the mess. "Cleaning up this mess will keep me busy, I guess. I find things more bearable if I stay busy."

We walked to the front door. I paused in the living room to admire the Chelsea Brass Marine clock on the mantel. The Shakespearean quote caught my eye again. "Time is the justice that examines all offenders." Indeed.

I started to leave, and Mrs. Hamilton touched my arm. I turned to her and she leaned against me and hugged me. I was taken by surprise, but I hugged her back.

"Thank you, Pete," she whispered. "May I call you Pete? I feel so alone, and you're the only one I can count on. Even James thinks Sidney took his own life. Thank you, Pete. Thank you."

135

My voice felt hoarse, but I muttered, "You're welcome, Lucille," and I left.

I talked to the neighbors on either side of the Hamilton home, but no one had seen or heard anything unusual that morning. One woman thought she might have seen a sedan parked on the street near the Hamilton house, but since it didn't look unusual she didn't recall any details. I reported my findings to Mrs. Hamilton before I left and drove back to my office.

The office was empty, but I knew where Agnes would be so I locked up and walked down the street. I found her sitting in the lobby of the Eaton Hotel reading the morning edition of the *Wichita Eagle*. I sat down beside her and glanced at the paper. She was reading a story about a performer who had died the day before during an air show in France. I read a few lines along with her. The man from Michigan was a young parachutist performing before 100,000 Frenchmen in Vincennes. Although he was young, he was experienced, but something went terribly wrong this day. The journalist who wrote the story had a flair for the melodramatic as he described the large crowd watching the young man frantically claw at the parachute that failed to open during his descent. They gasped and moaned in horror as he plunged to his death. I shuddered and picked up the sports section.

The Yankees had beaten the Red Sox nine to three in Boston. Malone was the winning pitcher, and Ferrell took the loss. The Yankee left fielder, Johnson, got three hits and knocked in a couple of runs. Lazzeri, the second baseman, had also knocked in a pair. These Yankees could hit and score runs, no doubt about it. I continued looking at the sports scores and spoke out of the corner of my mouth.

"What'd you find out, Agnes?"

Agnes rustled the paper and held it in front of her face.

"Our boy just came in. He's upstairs in his room. The desk clerk gave me the high sign when he came in so I know what he looks like now."

I glanced over at the desk clerk, a slightly built man in his mid-thirties with wire-rimmed glasses resting on a hooked beak. His face bore scars from a lost battle with teenage acne.

"Good for you, Agnes. Did you slip the desk clerk a buck to give you the nod?"

"No, he sensed something was up and held out for a Lincoln."

I whistled softly.

"Meier looked like a man with a purpose when he went upstairs," Agnes said. "He also didn't look like he intended to spend the rest of the day in his room."

"Yeah, I can imagine. I think I know where he's been, too."

Agnes gave me a puzzled look, but before I could say anything else she gave me the elbow and pointed her chin at a man striding through the lobby. Jonas Meier was a tall, slender man wearing a dark blue suit and a gray fedora. He looked to be in his forties. The hair at his temples was dark, salted with a bit of gray. He had dark eyes recessed deep into his skull, and he was one of those unfortunate guys with a heavy beard who always looked liked he needed a shave. He had a narrow scar that ran from just under his left eye to the corner of his mouth. His thin lips looked liked they would crack if he ever broke into a smile. The man looked like a wanted poster.

I stood up and folded the sports section under my arm and started to follow him. Agnes grabbed my elbow.

"Pete, wait," she said.

"You go back to the office, Agnes. I'll call as soon as I can, as soon as I find out what this guy is up to."

"Be careful, Pete," she said.

"Good advice, doll. Anything else?"

"Yeah, I haven't finished reading that paper," she said.

I handed her the paper and flashed a grin and headed out the door. Meier stood on the sidewalk next to the doorman. He had the doorman hail a taxi. Just before he got in the taxi, Meier lit a cigarette. He used his left hand to strike the match. I had the doorman hail the next cab for me.

"Follow that car," I said.

Meier's cab turned right at the corner then made another right and headed west. After a few blocks, it turned south on Broadway with my cab a few cars behind.

"You're doing fine," I said to the cabbie.

He nodded and gave me the thumbs up. I leaned back and lit a cigarette and kept my eyes on the windshield. We continued south for several blocks until we crossed the John Mack Bridge and got into the seedier section of town.

It was only the middle of the afternoon, but already several hookers were strolling on the sidewalks advertising their wares. We stopped at a light with one car separating Meier's cab from mine. A hooker on the sidewalk caught my eye and winked. She wasn't unattractive, but her best years were behind her. She had shoulder length blond hair, but a nickel would get your dime that the roots were dark. She bent over to adjust her hose, no doubt so I would notice her ample cleavage. It worked. I noticed. When she caught me staring she feigned modesty by covering her breasts with delicate fingers featuring bright, red nails. The light changed and we started to roll. The hooker gave me a pouty face and blew a kiss. Some women aren't virgins, I thought to myself, and some never were.

After a few more blocks, Meier's cab turned back to the east and stopped in front of a small shack that served as a tavern. A weathered sign over the doorway read "The Salty Dog." Its roof sagged, and it hadn't seen a coat of paint since Abner Doubleday threw out the first pitch. Meier got out of the cab and went inside. I waited a moment and did the same.

It took several seconds for my eyes to adjust to the dim lighting, and when they did I concluded that dim lighting was the best thing this place had going for it. I took a seat at the bar and ordered a bottle of beer. I didn't want to take a chance drinking beer from a glass. I took a swallow and turned slowly on my stool, surveying the room.

Along with a half dozen stools at the bar, four or five small tables filled the room. Meier sat at a table in the corner talking to another man in a suit whose back was to the room. The place was small, but I couldn't hear what they were saying. They sat with their heads close together. There were a few people sitting at tables closer to the bar and a man and woman sitting at the bar, all carrying on conversations that covered the voices from the corner.

I pulled my hat low over my eyes. I didn't want to be seen and didn't have to worry. The dim lighting served as a cover, and no one was paying attention to me anyway. Unfortunately, the same lighting prevented me from getting a good look at the table in the corner. Meier's tall, lanky frame was recognizable, but the man with his back to me was not. I could see a shorter, wider man whose silhouette I thought I recognized.

After a few moments, the conversation grew more heated. The shorter man became more animated, waving his arms and slamming a fist down on the table. Meier leaned over and spoke softly. The shorter man waved a finger at Meier who sat for a moment longer without speaking. Finally, Meier stood up and walked toward the exit leaving the shorter man behind. He ducked his head when he went through the door, a habit taller guys develop, and left the bar alone. I let him go and took another pull on my bottle of beer. I wanted to see if I could identify the other guy.

Three or four minutes passed before the guy looked at his watch and stood up. He was almost to the doorway before I got a look at his face. It was Gordon Veatch. I wasn't surprised, really, although I was surprised to find him in a dive like this. Why would Veatch meet Jonas Meier here of all places? Why wouldn't he meet with Meier in his office?

I thought about it, and the answer seemed obvious. Veatch didn't want anyone to know he was meeting Meier. Who would suspect Veatch of hanging around a joint like this? Meier wanted something Veatch had, and Veatch didn't want anyone to know he was dealing with Meier, and yours truly had played right into their hands. Veatch had me fingered as the bad guy or at least he would when he got his day in court. I'd already been nabbed for breaking and entering, and when the plans for the bomb sighting device couldn't be located, I'd be prosecuted for taking them. Veatch would have sold the plans to the Germans by then, and the truth would be buried with me in a prison cell.

Tuesday, May 4

I was talking to Agnes over breakfast at the Eaton Hotel. I was having a platter of scrambled eggs, bacon, hash brown potatoes, and toast washed down with several cups of black coffee. Agnes was picking at half a grapefruit and sipping on coffee with cream.

"Veatch is involved with this German Meier," I said. "How could he not be? Meier must be after the plans Ireland told me about, plans for a more developed and sophisticated sighting device to be used on bombers. According to Ireland, the military that owns these plans would have a distinct advantage over its enemies during times of war. He's probably right, but what do I know? Frankly, I don't give a damn about plans, planes, or bomb sighting devices. I only care about finding the murderer or murderers of Sidney Hamilton and Alice Bennett. The rest I'll leave for the aircraft executives to figure out."

"Could Gordon Veatch be such a rotten guy?" she asked. "He's in a top position with Stearman. Why would he get involved with something like this?"

I swallowed a bite of toast and nodded.

"That's a good question, Agnes, and I suppose the answer is money. He's a hard-nosed jerk, but the world is full of jerks. That doesn't make him a crook and a killer. I don't know. Maybe it has something to do with the Stearman merger with Boeing. Maybe

141

Boeing won't need a guy like Veatch around. He probably commands a hefty salary, and they may be loaded with guys like Veatch."

I recalled reading about the Boeing takeover of Stearman some months ago, but didn't know how long things like this took. Even after the takeover, I suspected the fallout from personnel changes would take months or even years. These things always brought opportunity for a few and the hatchet for many.

"Ireland is mixed up in this, too, but I don't know how deep," I said.

"You mean because he works for Veatch?" Agnes said.

"Yes and no. Remember I found Meier's name and number in Ireland's office. That's the clue that led me to the German in the first place. I don't know, though. Something doesn't add up. If the Germans want the plans for this device, and they must, they would want to keep everything as quiet as possible. They'd want a single contact. This isn't something a guy like Veatch would entrust to a guy like Ireland. Ireland strikes me as being less than brilliant. In fact, I suspect as an engineer he's incredibly average. He's been assigned to reconstruct Hamilton's work or find Hamilton's plans or design the device on his own. I doubt if Veatch cares which, but I think Ireland is coming up short. I'm sure he got the assignment only on the strength of his relationship with Hamilton in the first place, but I suspect Ireland just can't fill Hamilton's shoes. Still, if Veatch is working with Meier, I can't believe he'd include Ireland on that."

Agnes sipped her coffee and took out a cigarette. I leaned over and lit it for her and one for myself. She stared at the smoke for a moment before speaking.

"You know, Pete, you may be overlooking something here."

I chuckled.

"Hell, Agnes, I'm probably overlooking a lot."

"Yeah, well, that's probably true. You're assuming that Meier's contact is Veatch. You saw them together in a tavern."

I nodded.

"Suppose Veatch wasn't Meier's contact, at least at the beginning," she said. "Suppose he's only talking to Veatch now, because circumstances have forced him to."

I saw where she was going. I'd thought about this myself, but I didn't want to believe it.

"You could be right, Agnes," I said. "Meier had another contact at Stearman, someone willing to sell the plans at a price, someone who could deliver."

Agnes nodded and waited. I couldn't say his name so she filled it in for me.

"Someone like Sidney Hamilton," she said.

Neither of us spoke for several moments. We smoked in silence. Across the lobby, Waldo was popping his shine rag over the shoes of a man wearing a suit and reading the paper. I looked at my own shoes. I'd missed my usual Sunday morning shoeshine, and my shoes showed it. I glanced at the paper lying on our table. We'd read it earlier. It contained a report on the German Luftwaffe destroying the Basque town of Guernica, Spain last week.

"I've been wondering about Hamilton," I said. "He seems to have been the one with the brains to pull this off. After all, he created the plans. I can imagine Meier killing Hamilton, not wanting to leave any loose ends, but if he had the plans, and he killed Hamilton, why is he still here? Why would he hang around? No, if he had the plans, he would have left by now."

"Hamilton could have changed his mind," Agnes said.

"You're right. If he changed his mind, Meier would have killed him, but not right away. He would have tortured him first, tried to make him talk. And none of this explains why Alice Bennett was killed. I still believe the deaths are related, but how? Alice Bennett saw Sidney Hamilton return to his home on Tuesday morning the day he disappeared. Ten days later she was murdered. Why? How are the deaths connected?"

"Alice Bennett was the last to see Hamilton alive," Agnes said.

"Not quite. The last person to see Hamilton alive was his murderer."

Agnes nodded.

"So what's next?" she said.

"You stay here. Have another cup of coffee. Watch for Meier to leave his room. If he does, give me the high sign."

"Where are you going?"

"To get a shoeshine."

I left the dining room and crossed the lobby to Waldo's stand. The man in the suit had left, and the chair was empty. I took a seat as Waldo stared down at my shoes and said, "Yassuh."

"It's me, Waldo."

Waldo looked up and beamed.

"Good morning, Mr. Stone. I wondered when you were going to stop by. I missed you Sunday morning."

"Blame the sandman, Waldo. I woke up on Sunday morning, looked out the window, looked back at my bed, and climbed back under the sheets."

We both laughed.

"I want to thank you, Mr. Stone."

"For what?"

Waldo smiled and popped his rag.

"I appreciate it, Mr. Stone. What you did was nice."

"You're welcome, Waldo. How's Ralph doing?"

He didn't look up, but he shook his head.

"I just don't know about that boy. He seems to be drawn to trouble. Right now he's angry, angry at losing his job. What you did was the right thing, Mr. Stone, and I appreciate it, I really do, but the boy doesn't see it that way. He was making good money, and now he isn't so he's angry."

"Hmm, yeah, I understand. I don't suppose I could talk to him."

"You could try, but he probably won't talk to you. God knows he won't talk to me. He's hanging around a pool hall on Oliver near College Hill running errands for the swells. He's there late afternoons and evenings when the stuffed shirts stop by to shoot a little pool at the end of a day. That boy sure knows the smell of money."

"I'll see if I can stop by," I said.

Waldo finished the shine, and I reached for my wallet, but he stopped me.

"This one's on the house," he said.

I started to protest, but I could see he meant it, and I didn't want to hurt his feelings, so I thanked him and went back into the dining room. Agnes was sipping coffee and reading the paper and exhibiting the patience of an experienced detective.

"Anything on our friend, Meier?" I said.

"Not a thing. He hasn't come down yet."

"Are we sure he's in his room?"

"I spoke to the night clerk before he went off duty. He said Meier went to his room last night at about nine o'clock and never came down. Same with the day clerk, and I've been here since he came on duty. I haven't seen Meier either. He's in his room. I asked the maid if she'd seen anything, and she said the 'Do Not Disturb' sign is on his door. Guess he's sleeping in."

I checked my watch. The morning was nearly gone.

"Okay, good work, Agnes. Can you stand waiting for a bit longer? I want to know what Meier's next move is. When he comes down, tail him and call the office as soon as you see anything."

"Are you going back to the office?"

"Just for a minute, but I have some people I want to see. I'll check in with the answering service to see if you've left a message."

"Okay," she said. "I can wait. I gave the clerk a buck to watch for Meier when I have to visit the powder room, and I gave the maid another dollar to let me know when Meier stirs. Everybody has their hand out. I had no idea this line of work required such an outlay of cash."

I grinned and pulled some bills out of my wallet and handed them to Agnes.

"Money keeps the wheels greased," I said. "Don't worry. It will all be worth it."

I gave her a peck on the forehead and left her to her detecting. I walked back to the office and made a phone call and checked for messages. There were none so I left and drove to the police station. I found McCormick in his office giving an earful to a rookie cop who'd had the audacity to give a parking ticket to a city commissioner. The rookie left Mac's office shaking, having learned a valuable lesson about to whom the law applies and to whom it does not. I walked in after the rookie walked out. McCormick sat at his desk biting down on a cigar stub.

"Jesus, Stone," he said. "The Dodgers lost another one, I ran over my wife's cat this morning, and my hemorrhoids are on fire. Why wouldn't you show up today?"

"Nice to see you, too, Mac."

"Get out of my office."

I ignored that and took the chair in front of his desk.

"I have information on the case," I said.

"Which case? The Bennett murder?"

"The Hamilton murder," I said.

"You mean the Hamilton suicide. Jesus, Stone, you never give up, do you? Okay, what have you got?"

I took out a cigarette and lit it.

"Gordon Veatch is dirty," I said. "He's dealing with the Germans."

McCormick stared at me for a moment like I was a lunatic. Then he leaned back and laughed, a real guffaw.

"Say, Stone, you get to me. You really do. In a few days Veatch is going to see you in court, and when he does he's going to convince a judge that you are not only a crook, which you are, but a serious threat to the security of our country, which I find hard to believe, but I'd hate to be your lawyer and have to prove otherwise. So what do you do? The only sensible thing, you accuse Veatch of being the bad guy. Not bad, Stone, not bad. The old 'turn the tables' trick. Get out of here, Stone. You've only got a few days left. Go detect or whatever it is you do. Leave me alone. You're a pain in the ass, and that's something I really don't need right now."

McCormick shifted uneasily in his chair, and I saw that he was sitting on an overstuffed pillow. Evidently his hemorrhoids really were on fire.

"What about the Bennett murder?" I said. "The two deaths are connected. Is there anything new?"

Mac sighed and ran his fingers through his hair and shook his head.

"We've got nothing, Stone, nothing, and if you have anything on that murder, the Wichita Police Department would look kindly upon you if you would share it. There's no witness, no motive. We've questioned the husband again and again. He has an ironclad alibi."

"Did he have her killed?"

Mac stared at me, and his face grew dark.

"We thought about that," he said, "but again, there was no motive. They had a happy marriage, no sign that either one was fooling around. Hell, she wasn't even insured, so it couldn't have been for money. What we've got is a big, fat zero."

"The deaths are connected," I said.

"So you keep saying, and maybe you're right, but how? Let's suppose you are right about Hamilton being murdered, which you aren't. How would his death, at the hands of Veatch, is that right? How would his death at the hands of Veatch have anything to do with the murder of Alice Bennett? I suppose Veatch killed Hamilton, and as long as he was in the neighborhood he killed Bennett, too. Except that Hamilton didn't die at his home. He died in the river, which is not in the neighborhood. And Bennett didn't die when Hamilton did. She was murdered ten days later. Why? Answer me that, Stone, and you'll earn my undying respect and admiration. Until then, you are just a crook out on bail, and you're wasting my time. Get out of here."

McCormick made a face as he shifted in his chair again before waving the back of his hand at me. I left.

I walked out of the police station and stopped at a pay phone on the corner. I dropped a nickel and dialed the number for the Eaton Hotel. When the operator answered, I asked for Agnes and waited for her to be paged. A couple of minutes later she came on the line.

"Hey, kid," I said, "what do you know?"

"Well, I've gotten through the sports pages and managed to memorize every baseball score from yesterday's games. I can also recite more than a few of the players' batting averages, but as for Meier there's nothing, Pete, absolutely nothing. He's still holed up in his room. He hasn't budged. I snuck up to the fourth floor about twenty minutes ago, and the 'Do Not Disturb' sign is still on the door."

I glanced at my watch. Something was wrong. Meier wouldn't still be in bed unless he was sick, or worse.

"Sit tight, Agnes. I'll be there in a few minutes."

I hung up the phone and drove to the Eaton. Agnes was sitting in the dining room at the table where I'd left her. I gave her a nod and walked to the front desk. A pimply-faced young man was on duty.

"Give me the key to Room 409," I said.

He searched the rows of keys hanging on the wall and turned to me.

"That room is taken, sir. I'm sorry, but I can't give you a key."

"I know the room is taken," I said, "but something is wrong. I need to get into the room, now."

The kid threw back his shoulders.

"Say, are you trying to be a tough guy?" he said. "You can't just go into another man's room."

"Listen you little twit, I've got to get into that room. If you don't give me a key in the next two seconds, I'm going to put in a call to the city police, and they'll turn this place into a three ring circus. Is that what your boss would want?"

That let the air out of his balloon.

"Okay, okay, no need to blow your wig. I can't give you a key, but I can open the door with a passkey. You better know what you're doing, mister."

I didn't have any idea what I was doing, but I wasn't going to clue in the punk. We took the elevator together to the fourth floor and walked down the hall to Room 409. The sign still hung on the door. The kid read it to me.

"This sign says 'Do Not Disturb.'"

"Great line, Shakespeare," I said. "Now open the door."

The kid shook his head, but he knew I meant business. He knocked first and called Meier's name. There was no answer. He knocked a second time with the same result. The kid looked at me, and I nodded at the lock. He put the passkey in and opened the door.

149

The first thing that hit me was the smell, a distinct coppery odor that hit my nostrils and triggered raw memories, none of them good. The blinds were drawn, and the windows were down. The room was dark and stuffy. The clerk flicked on a lamp and gasped.

Meier lay supine on the bed soaked in blood. His eyes were open, and he stared at the ceiling, but I was certain he saw nothing. The bullet hole in the middle of his forehead convinced me of that. I turned his head to the side and noted that the hole in the back of his head was much larger. Meier was dressed in his suit, and a German luger lay in his right hand.

"Go downstairs and call the police," I said. "Ask for Lieutenant McCormick. Have you got that?"

The kid kept staring at the corpse. I turned him toward me and shook his shoulders.

"Have you got that?" I said.

He nodded with his mouth hung open.

"Yeah, yeah, call the police. Ask for McDermott."

"Not McDermott, you idiot! McCormick. McCormick."

The kid stared at me.

"McCormick," he said. "Got it."

He left the room which is what I wanted. I went through Meier's pockets first and found some change, a cigarette lighter, and a few wrapped peppermints. I left all of that there. His wallet was in the breast pocket of his suit coat. It contained several hundred dollars in cash and some identification. I left that intact, too. Behind the wallet was an appointment book. I glanced at it quickly and stuffed it in my pocket.

On a small table by the bed, I found a note. I couldn't read it, it was written in German, but I figured it was a suicide note. I took my book out of my pocket and copied the words into it. I studied the note's handwriting for a moment before putting it back on the table.

I checked the closet and desk drawers and found nothing of interest. When I finished, I sat down in the chair next to the desk and lit a cigarette and waited for the police to arrive. I didn't have to wait long. Apparently, the desk clerk had managed to snap out of it and make the call. McCormick strode into the room first, a couple of uniforms close behind. McCormick eyeballed the scene and whistled softly. He shifted his gaze toward me.

"Stone, it seems like every time there's a suspicious death these days, you are hovering nearby. Why is that?"

I puffed on my cigarette and shrugged.

"Just part of my charm, I guess."

"Yeah, well, I wish you'd peddle your charm in another city. You're giving me a headache. Talk to me, Stone. What do you know about this?"

"The victim's name is Jonas Meier. He's German. I don't know how long he's been in Wichita. I've been tailing him for a couple of days now. I think he was involved in the aircraft industry. I don't know why, and I don't know how, but I also think he was involved in the murder of Sidney Hamilton."

"Why should a German involved in the aircraft industry be a suspect for murder? Is this the guy you claim was dealing with Veatch? What else do you know, Stone? Does this guy have anything to do with your breaking into the Stearman offices? How the hell is any of this your business?"

"Frankly, I don't give a damn what Meier was doing in Wichita except that he may have been involved in the death of Sidney Hamilton. If he was, I intend to find out."

McCormick shook his head.

"Sidney Hamilton, Sidney Hamilton," he said. "Are you ever going to let that rest?"

I stared at McCormick and didn't say a thing.

"Okay," he said, "tell me how you discovered the body. Tell me everything, Stone, and don't leave anything out."

I told McCormick about how I'd tailed Meier, how he'd met with Gordon Veatch. I didn't tell him how I'd come to learn about Meier in the first place, by breaking into James Ireland's office. He wasn't satisfied, and he didn't hide it. I'd have to answer to him later, but at the moment he had more pressing business.

"How did you discover the body? Were you breaking and entering, again?"

The desk clerk tried to speak, and Mac shut him up with a glare.

"When Meier didn't show this morning, I sensed something was wrong," I said. "The desk clerk and I entered the room together and found him lying on the bed just like this."

I nodded toward the bed.

"I had the clerk call you as soon as we discovered the body."

"Yeah, I'll bet you did," Mac said. "You had the clerk call me while you tossed the room."

I feigned shock and innocence. Mac didn't buy it.

"What do you make of the death?" Mac said.

"Bullet to the forehead, German luger in his hand…" I said.

"Suicide?" Mac said.

I shrugged.

"Is there a note?" Mac said. "And don't try to tell me you haven't looked. If you tell me that, Stone, I'll personally run you downtown and throw you in a cell."

I nodded toward the small table. McCormick picked up the note and held it under a lamp.

"It's in German," he said and stuffed it into his pocket. "I'll have to find someone to translate it."

McCormick nodded and stared at the body for several long moments.

"Is this a suicide or did someone want to make it look like a suicide?" Mac said. He looked at me and raised his eyebrows. "What else is in the room?"

"Nothing special," I said, "clothes, shaving kit, the usual."

The county coroner arrived and examined the body and declared him dead. Imagine that. How would we have known if the coroner hadn't arrived? I put on my hat and headed for the door. McCormick called out to me.

"Stay close, Stone. This isn't over. I want to talk to you about this."

I gave him a wave and left.

♦ ♦ ♦

"Jonas Meier is dead."

"So I gathered," Agnes said, "when I watched the cops, the coroner, and a stretcher go up in the elevator."

"I knew you were a detective," I said.

We were back in the office. I filled Agnes in on the details, telling her what I discovered when the desk clerk opened the door.

"So it's a suicide," Agnes said.

I stroked my chin.

"That's what McCormick is calling it."

"You don't sound convinced."

"I have my doubts, Agnes, but it's just a theory. I think McCormick has doubts, too, probably because he knows I do."

I reached into my pocket for the appointment book I'd lifted from Meier's room. There were a few notations in German under the next few dates, but Thursday, May 6th was circled. That was the day after tomorrow. Written beneath the date were the letters HLNASt. The first five letters were capitalized, but the 't' was in lower case. Was it someone's name? H. L. Nast? I had no idea.

"So what are you going to do?" Agnes said.

I put the appointment book back in my pocket.

"I'm going to see a man about translating some German. Hold down the fort, Agnes."

"It's a suicide note, alright. It doesn't say anything special, and it's not addressed to anyone. Just the usual: I can't go on, life is meaningless. Where did this come from?"

I was in James Ireland's office. I recalled from the yearbook Mrs. Hamilton had given me that both Ireland and Hamilton had been members of the German club when they were in college together. I was betting he could translate the note, and I was correct. Ireland seemed fluent in the language.

I ignored his question about the source of the note. I pulled the appointment book from my pocket and opened it.

"How about the name H. L. Nast? Do you know anyone by that name?"

Ireland shook his head.

"How about Thursday, May 6th? Is there any reason why that date is special?"

"There's nothing special about May 6th as far as I know," he said.

I opened the book to today's date and held it in front of Ireland.

"How about this? Anything special in here?"

He looked at me with a curious expression and began reading silently while I held the book in front of his face.

"There's nothing in particular here, just a list of errands. Here he was out of shaving cream, over here he wrote down cigarettes. Here are some initials: G.V. Who's G.V.? Gordon Veatch?"

"That would be my guess," I said.

"None of this means a thing to me," Ireland said. "It might help if I knew what this was about. Where did that note come from? Whose book is this?"

"I found them in Jonas Meier's room," I said, "along with one very dead Jonas Meier."

I watched Ireland carefully to gauge his reaction. He didn't look shocked or surprised.

"Jonas Meier?" he asked. "Should I know Jonas Meier?"

Ireland was playing dumb. I played along with him.

"I was in the Eaton Hotel when his body was discovered. I happened to be one of the first people in his room. I had hoped to talk to Meier. I thought he might know something about the death of Sidney Hamilton."

"Say, that's a stretch, isn't it, Mr. Stone? How could this Jonas Meier be involved with Sidney's death?"

"Frankly, I don't know. I don't know if they were connected at all. I'm just bumbling around, scratching and kicking and peeking into crevices. Something will turn up."

"Are you sure, Mr. Stone?"

"No, I'm never sure, but that's usually what happens. Someone makes a mistake, something doesn't smell right, or someone cracks. It may take a while, but something will turn up. I'll keep sniffing around until it does. Thanks for the German lesson, Mr. Ireland."

Ireland had played it cool, alright. He'd acted like he didn't even know who Meier was. Why? Did he have something to hide or was he under orders from Veatch to keep mum. I didn't know, but I filed it away and decided I needed to talk to Veatch. That wasn't going to be easy since Veatch hated my guts, and I was probably the last guy he wanted to talk to. Anyone in my position who had any brains would stay out of Veatch's way. Well, the only guy in my position was me, and I'd never claimed to be a Rhodes Scholar. I was going to talk to him.

The shadows on the sidewalk were growing long. I checked my watch and realized the day was nearly gone. It was almost six o'clock. I found a pay phone and called the office. Agnes answered on the first ring.

"Agnes, why are you still at the office?"

"You left and told me to hold down the fort. I'm holding it down."

"I'm going to have to choose my words more carefully, Agnes. You're a doll. Did anyone call?"

"Lieutenant McCormick called about an hour ago. He wants you to stop by the station. That's it."

"Okay. Thanks, Agnes. Now go home and get some rest. I'll see you tomorrow."

Thaddeus McCormick wanted to see me, but I didn't want to see him, at least not now. I was, however, the last person Gordon Veatch wanted to see. That wasn't a great reason to visit his office, but it would have to do.

I pulled up in front of the Stearman offices and glanced at my watch. It read twenty minutes after six o'clock. There was only one car in the parking lot, a Cadillac. I recalled seeing the same car in the parking lot at The Salty Dog. It had to belong to Veatch.

Guys like Gordon Veatch don't make it to the top by working from nine to five. I suspected he would still be at his office working alone, and that's the way I wanted it. I didn't need a gatekeeper secretary stalling my entrance or calling the police.

The hangar area was lit but quiet. Everyone had gone home. The front door to the offices was unlocked. I walked in and went past the reception area and paused outside Veatch's office. I didn't hear anything, but a light shone from under the door. I turned the knob and walked in.

Veatch was sitting at his desk in his overstuffed chair. His shirt sleeves were rolled up and his tie was loosened. He had a fat cigar stuck in the corner of his mouth. He was looking over some engineering drawings spread over his desk. His eyebrows went up when he saw me, but to his credit he didn't look panicked or nervous. I was on his turf, and he was in control.

"What the hell are you doing here, Stone?"

"I was going to ask you the same question. Aren't your offices closed?"

Veatch leaned forward a bit and took the cigar out of his mouth.

"Do they look closed? Listen carefully, you son of a bitch. When my ass is in this chair, the offices of Stearman Aircraft are open."

I forced myself not to smile.

"Now get the hell out of here," he said, "before I call the police."

I reached over and picked up his phone.

"Call them. That'll give you a chance to explain why you killed Jonas Meier."

Either Veatch was a great actor or the look of surprise on his face was genuine.

"What are you talking about?"

"Come on, Veatch. You know what I'm talking about. Jonas Meier, your Teutonic business associate, was found dead in his hotel room today. Don't act so surprised."

"Business associate?" he said. "What the hell are you talking about, Stone? Business associate? I assure you I am no associate of Jonas Meier."

He was a good actor.

"Nice try, Veatch. I saw the two of you together yesterday, and Meier was found dead today. You two were head to head in a dump called The Salty Dog. The conversation looked pretty heated. Would you like to explain to Wichita's finest why you were having a tete-a-tete with a German who showed up dead the following day?"

"Careful, Stone. In less than a week, I intend to see you brought to court on charges of breaking and entering, theft, sedition, and any other crime our lawyers can think of. You keep talking like this, and I'll add slander to the charges."

"I know what I saw, Veatch. You can deny it all you want, but I'll tell my story to Lieutenant McCormick downtown, and I'll make him believe it."

"I don't deny I met with Meier. I did. That doesn't make me his associate."

"How about Nast? Know anybody by that name?"

Veatch screwed up his brow.

"Who?" he said. "Did you say Nast? I don't know what you're talking about."

"Look, Mr. Veatch. I'm on to something. I don't know what, but I intend to find out who killed Sidney Hamilton. It's possible that this Jonas Meier was the killer. I need more time to prove it. Just back off on your charges, at least for a few more days until I figure this out."

"Hah, fat chance, gumshoe. I'm not backing off of anything. You're a criminal, Stone, and you deserve to be put away. I'll see you in court on Monday."

"Why were you talking to Jonas Meier?"

"That's none of your business, Stone. Nothing that happens at Stearman Aircraft is any of your business."

"I take exception to that remark. I've been hired to find the murderer of Sidney Hamilton, one of your former employees. I would think you'd be interested in that, Mr. Veatch. Why aren't you interested?"

"Listen, Stone. The police have ruled Hamilton's death a suicide. As difficult as it is, I accept that explanation. All you have done and all you are doing is taking advantage of a widow and getting in the way of our business. I'm going to say this one more time, and then I'm calling the police. Get out, Stone, and stay out."

We glared at each other for several seconds before I turned on my heel and left.

I was hot. I had tossed my last chip into the pot, and I wasn't even holding a pair. My meeting with Veatch to plea for more time to work on the case had been a long shot that didn't pay off.

I decided a cold beer would cool me off, so I drove across town to Tom's Inn. It looked pretty quiet, and that's the way I wanted it. I nodded at Tom went I came through the door, and he had a draw waiting at the bar when I sat down. Mabel stuck her head around the corner and asked if I was hungry. I shook my head 'no,' and she disappeared into the kitchen. Larry the mechanic sat at the other end of the bar, and next to him was a huge figure I recognized as Leonard. They nodded when I sat down, and I gave them a polite wave, but I didn't join them. I needed some time alone to work things out in my mind. Tom sensed I didn't want to chat, so he drew my beer and moved down to the other end of the bar wiping it with his rag as he went.

A couple of cold ones brought me out of my funk, and when Tom set the next one down in front of me, I told him to pour one for himself. He did.

"You look like you've lost your best friend," he said.

"I feel like I never had one," I said with a shrug. "I feel like the bug under a fat man's heel. Heard any baseball scores today?"

"Yeah, the Yankees beat the Tigers ten to one in Detroit."

"And the fat man crushes another bug," I said.

"Hey, don't look to me to cheer you up," Tom said.

He moved to the end of the bar to pick up the empty glasses in front of Leonard and Larry. I motioned to Tom to put their refills on my tab, and he did. The big guys waved their appreciation, and I waved back. We talked baseball some more, and the hour grew late.

"One more, Tom," I said, "then it's home for me."

Tom drew another beer, and a pair of tough-looking mugs came through the door. I watched them in the mirror behind the bar. They squeezed into a booth behind me. They wore dark suits with hats down pulled low. One of them was a bit taller and darker than the other, and I picked up a bulge in his jacket where a shoulder holster would ride. The shorter one had sandy hair peeking from beneath his hat. He was stockier than his taller companion, but the extra weight was all muscle. He was turned slightly with his back to the room, and I couldn't tell for sure, but I figured he was packing, too.

Tom served them each a beer and returned to the bar.

"Ever see those two in here before?" I said.

Tom looked in their direction and shook his head.

"No, never seen them," he said.

I glanced down the bar toward Leonard and Larry and looked back to the images in the mirror.

"I feel like I'm in the land of giants," I said.

Tom nodded and grinned. I eyed the pair in the booth and swallowed the last of my beer. They sat quietly and sipped their beers. Neither had said a word since Tom brought their drinks. I tossed a couple of bills on the bar and tipped a finger toward Tom.

"Goodnight," I said and waved to Larry and Leonard at the other end of the bar.

I walked to my roadster and started to get in, when I was braced by the pair from inside. Why wasn't I surprised? The shorter, heavier one grabbed my right arm, from behind, and the taller one squeezed my left arm.

"Geez, fellas," I said. "It's a beautiful night, but I'm just too tired to dance. Maybe another night, OK?"

The taller one spoke.

"A real wise guy, huh. Looks like Mr. Dexter was right. He said you were a wise acre, a smart guy. Well maybe this will keep your yammering down."

A punch landed in my gut with a force somewhere similar to that of a sledge hammer or a runaway Buick. I felt the air go out and watched the stars and the moon spin above me. Just when I thought the beer I'd been drinking was about to come up, another fist slammed into my jaw followed by another just above my eye. Neither man had loosened his grip on my arms. At this point it really didn't matter. I figured one more punch was all I could take, and I was right. Another fist landed under my chin, and I watched the starry, starry night fade away.

Wednesday, May 5

The city woke to a sky full of clouds, and a dark one hung over me. It felt like it weighed a ton. I struggled to open my eyes and found myself in a room at once familiar and strange to me. The walls were covered with floral-patterned wallpaper, and the scent of lilac wafted through the room. I lay staring at the ceiling and tried to piece together the events that brought me here, but I couldn't concentrate. My head was too sore, and the pain was too great. It felt like a heavyweight fighter was going a few rounds with a punching bag behind my eyeballs. My jaw ached, and when I touched it lightly I could tell it was swollen. I didn't bother touching my nose. I was sure it was broken. My arms ached, but when I flexed my fingers, they felt fine. Someone had done a number on me, alright, and apparently I hadn't landed a punch.

I heard a doorknob turn, and someone stepped into the room. From the other side of the door the aroma of fresh coffee mingled with the smell of lilac. I preferred the smell of the coffee. I continued staring at the ceiling, too tired and sore to turn my head until a face appeared above mine. The face belonged to Agnes, and her smile lifted the cloud.

"Well, darling," she whispered. "I thought I'd never get you back into my bed, and, yet, here you are. How are you feeling?"

I tried my voice and could manage only a hoarse whisper.

"Never better, sweetheart, although if this condition is due to our lovemaking, I'm calling a halt to our romance."

Agnes tried to laugh, but she got teary-eyed instead.

"Oh, Pete, you look like hell. Those guys really did a number on you."

I closed my eyes and replayed the previous night's events in my mind.

"How did I get here, Agnes? The last thing I remember was collapsing in a heap outside Tom's bar."

"Tom brought you here, right after he picked you up off the sidewalk. Two guys from the bar took care of the goons who did this to you."

"That would have been Leonard and Larry. Boy, do I owe them."

"That sounds, right," Agnes said. "I believe Tom mentioned those names. It must have been quite a brawl. The police hauled off the men who beat you. They're cooling their heels in jail. McCormick wants you to stop in as soon as you're able to make a statement."

"How about Leonard and Larry? How did they fare?"

"A few cuts and bruises, but they gave a lot better than they got. According to what they said, it looked like the goons were just getting started on you. Apparently, Leonard and Larry left the bar as soon as they saw the goons follow you out. My god, Pete, what would have happened if they hadn't been there? You could have been killed."

Agnes dabbed at her eyes with a handkerchief.

"I called the doctor as soon as Tom brought you here. You were mumbling something about not wanting to go to the hospital, but you were pretty much out of it. The doctor gave you some pain medication and bandaged you up. Your nose is broken, but nothing else is, although I'm sure you'll be sore for a few days."

Agnes leaned over and kissed my forehead.

"Would you like some breakfast?"

I shook my head slightly.

"I couldn't eat, Agnes, but that coffee smells good."

"Coming right up."

After she left the room, I spent the next day or so trying to stand up. At least it seemed that long. By the time Agnes returned with the coffee I had my legs all the way over the edge of the bed.

"Maybe you should just stay right here for a day or two, Pete."

"No can do, Agnes. You're a doll, but I've got to get back to work. That cup of plasma you're holding is just what I need."

And it was. I drank the coffee and had a cigarette. Getting dressed was a slow, agonizing chore, but with Agnes helping me, we got it done. I thanked her and kissed her, and she held me close for a long moment. I eased out the door and got into my car and drove to my place.

Taking a shower was a chore, but I managed it, and I climbed into a clean shirt and suit. I ached, but I was alive, and I had places to go and things to do.

I left my place and drove to the police station. I got to McCormick's office and made a statement against Reginald Dexter and his henchmen. Mac listened carefully without interrupting, and when I finished he barked into his phone, and a sergeant appeared in the doorway.

"Swear out a warrant against Reginald Dexter. Get some men and a couple of cars and find him. Arrest him and bring him in now."

The sergeant left without a word, and McCormick turned to me.

"Well, Stone, I could say you look like hell, but even a dope like you can see that. My advice to you is to avoid all mirrors for a few days. I could call you a stupid son-of-a-bitch, but I'd be wasting my breath. It's obvious nobody can beat any sense into you."

That was for openers. What followed was a royal butt chewing. I figured, why not? That was the only part of my anatomy that didn't ache at that particular moment.

He wanted to know what I knew about Jonas Meier, and I told him most of it, but I didn't mention the appointment book. I wasn't sure why I didn't mention it or the notation about H.L. Nast on May the 6th. I guess I reasoned that I was the only person other than Mrs. Hamilton, Lucille, who believed Sidney Hamilton was murdered. Why give McCormick all the information when he would just throw it back in my face? Now he believed Meier had committed suicide, too. Sure, there was a note, but what of it? Any Joe can write a note. I had evidence that Meier was left handed. The writing in his appointment book had the backward slant of a lefty. It didn't match the handwriting on the note. The gun we found was in Meier's right hand. Who shoots himself with his non-dominant hand? And who shoots himself in the forehead? It's easier to place the barrel at the temple and pull the trigger. Meier was murdered, I was sure of it. Was he killed for murdering Hamilton or did Hamilton's murderer kill Meier, too? Or was he killed for another reason entirely?

McCormick finished his tirade and waved me away with his customary back-handed swipe. I was only too happy to leave.

I drove by the Orpheum on North Broadway. They were playing *Mr. Deeds Goes to Town* with Gary Cooper and Jean Arthur. That Gary Cooper sure could act, and Jean Arthur was nice to look at. I made a mental note to ask Agnes if she would like to go to the movie with me. She'd been working hard and deserved a break.

As soon as I thought of Agnes, Mrs. Hamilton popped into my mind—or rather Lucille. Ever since she'd given me that hug in her living room, I'd begun thinking of her as Lucille, and I confessed to myself that I had been thinking about her a lot lately, too much, maybe. She was my client, and I needed to remember that.

I looked at my watch and saw that the morning was shot. My head hurt and so did my jaw, but the rumble in my stomach said I needed something to fill it. I stopped at a pay phone on the corner and called Agnes at the office. I told her I wouldn't be in today. I needed time to think. I drove west toward the river over the bumpy brick street. The top was down on my roadster, and I glanced up at the sky. Still cloudy, but it didn't look like rain.

In the distance I could see Lawrence Stadium. Pennants were flying, and it looked like a ballgame was getting underway. I do some of my best thinking at a ballgame surrounded by the buzz of the crowd and the chatter on the field. I figured, why not? I wasn't feeling spry at the moment, and sitting in the bleachers sounded like a better proposition than pounding the streets. A few minutes later I had parked my roadster and was walking into the stadium.

I bought a ticket and a program at the window, grabbed a hot dog and a beer at the concession stand, and took my seat behind the first base dugout. I took a bite of the dog. I was pleased to discover that working my jaw made it feel better.

The Wichita Watermen were hosting the Arkansas City Dubbs. I filled out the lineups on my scorecard and looked out over the field while the teams warmed up. The Watermen had finished batting practice, and several players were on the field stretching and getting limber for the contest. They wore white uniforms trimmed in blue, but most of the white had faded to a yellowish-gray hue. The Dubbs wore darker uniforms trimmed in red. Their team was still taking batting practice and warming up on the infield. A few players from each team huddled along the foul lines and chatted together.

It had been a while since I'd been in Lawrence Stadium, too long I figured. I thought back to last year when President Roosevelt had visited our city. It caused quite a stir. It was in October after the baseball season, but the president had used the stadium to make a campaign speech. Kansans' feelings toward Roosevelt were mixed, and he was running against our own Alf Landon. Frankly, I didn't much care one way or the other which politician sat in the White House. I've never cared much for politics, but I did get a front row seat to the Roosevelt's show.

Lieutenant McCormick and I were on better terms back then, and on that October day when the president visited, McCormick invited me to become a member of Wichita's finest, for exactly twenty-fours. The President of the United States had the Secret Service travelling with him at all times, but he still expected and required local law enforcement to assist in providing security. McCormick needed a few men to beef up his own force, so I was sworn in for the day.

I don't recall much of what Roosevelt said that day. I doubt if I was even listening. I do recall what I saw, the hoopla and fanfare surrounding his car and cavalcade. The stands were overflowing, and whatever animosity anyone felt toward the man, on that sunny fall day everyone cheered and whistled as he rode into view.

A stage and podium had been erected on the infield just in front of the pitcher's mound, and red, white, and blue bunting had been draped over the back side of the stage. I happened to have been stationed nearby between the pitcher's mound and second base.

The president's car drove to the rear of the structure that was encased in drapery. I watched as his aides lifted him out of the car and up onto the platform all out of sight of the crowd. They placed Roosevelt's crutches under his arms, and when he nodded they backed away. Using his crutches, the president appeared through the drapery and walked the two steps necessary to reach the podium. The entire maneuver took no more than a minute, and even though everyone present knew that Roosevelt had been stricken with polio as a younger man, and everyone knew that Roosevelt walked with the aid of crutches, what everyone saw was a healthy, robust world leader waving and smiling at the now standing crowd of cheering Kansans. What we see isn't always what is.

It was early in the baseball season now, and the players were a bit rusty. The match turned into a poorly pitched slugfest. Several errors added to the chaos. Wichita's shortstop, McElroy, booted a routine ground ball in the second inning, and the third baseman, Vicar, dropped a Texas League popup in the fourth and threw a ball over the head of the first baseman an inning later allowing a run to score. The shortstop for the Dubbs, not to be outdone, added a couple of errors on his own.

Still, both teams played hard, if not well, and each team collected twelve hits and two home runs. When the dust settled, Wichita prevailed with sixteen runs over Arkansas City's nine. None of the players on the field had a shot at playing in the big leagues, but there were glimpses of talent. In spite of McElroy's error at shortstop, he worked well with Bonder playing second base, and the pair turned four double plays over the course of the afternoon. The last double play came in the ninth inning and ended the game.

I mentioned something about the final play to a guy sitting next to me as he stood up to leave.

"It sure is a pleasure to see a couple of guys work together like that. It's almost like they each know what the other is thinking," I said.

"Sure, why wouldn't they," the guy said. "They've played together since they were kids, McElroy and Bonder have. You'd never believe they can't stand to be around each other off the field."

I raised my eyebrows and looked up at the guy.

"Is that right?" I said. "Why's that do you suppose?"

The guy sat back down and leaned over to fill me in.

"It started a couple of years ago, don't you know, about the time they started playing here in Wichita. They played together in Salina before this, and when they got here, they were still best of buddies. One of them met a dame, McElroy I believe it was, and he flipped over her. Trouble was Bonder met her, and he flipped over her, too. The dame dumped McElroy and gave Bonder a tumble, and that's when the trouble started."

"They play so well together on the field," I said. "You'd never know they don't get along off the field."

"Oh, they keep their problems off the field, alright," the guy said.

"How about the dame? Is she still Bonder's girl?"

"Are you nuts?" the guy said. "She left Bonder and ran off with a jazz musician from Kansas City. The only thing left of her is the bad blood between McElroy and Bonder. Can you believe that? A lousy dame drove a wedge between the best double-play combination this town has ever seen. Ah, what are you gonna do?"

The guy touched the bill of his hat and left. I finished writing the totals on my scorecard while the stands cleared out and thought about what he'd told me. The story wasn't new. History was full of guys, friends, and buddies, who'd had a falling out over a woman. The amazing thing was McElroy and Bonder still worked together as a team and kept their differences off the field.

The janitors started sweeping the stands and picking up the trash. I read over my completed scorecard and dropped it in a trash barrel as I left the stadium. I was only a few blocks from Tom's Inn, and I needed a place to think. I also needed a beer. I decided Tom's would do for both and steered the roadster in that direction.

◆ ◆ ◆

I sat at the end of the bar and sipped on a cold draft beer while I stared into the mirror behind the bar. The guy staring back at me looked older than I remembered him. The bruises and broken nose didn't help, but what I saw was age. A little gray showed in the temples, and bags hung below the eyes. What used to be called laugh lines around the eyes and mouth now just looked like plain old wrinkles. Mostly, the guy in the mirror looked tired, really tired. I thought about my age. In just over three weeks I would be forty-three years old, and more and more I was convinced this was a young man's game.

Murder is a particularly nasty business. It's not uncommon. It happens every day somewhere in the country, but that doesn't make it less loathsome. First degree murder requires cold-blooded planning and preparation. The killer must think through every step and consider each detail meticulously. I wondered how many potential murderers stopped right there, unable to get past the planning stage. Probably a lot of them.

After planning and preparation comes the most difficult part, executing the deed. It's the execution that separates the truly heartless from the pretenders. Far more murders are wished for and planned than are ever committed. It's the execution of murder that requires a human being to be cold, unfeeling, and reptilian, if only for that brief moment needed to strike, to kill.

Finally, the killer must not leave a clue as to who committed the crime. Not a weapon, not a footprint, not a thread of clothing or a hair off his head. Nothing can be left behind. Of course this is rarely the case, and, of course, murderers are rarely successful. If they were, guys like me would be out of business. Too many things can go wrong. Too many errors are made, human errors. For in the final analysis, as heinous as the crime is, murder is the most human of all crimes, committed by human beings against other human beings, and human beings are wired to make mistakes.

Sidney Hamilton's murderer made several mistakes. This killer covered his tracks alright. He was meticulous; he wasn't sloppy. It wasn't in his nature to be sloppy. He did, however, miscalculate one thing. He didn't count on a tenacious widow who wouldn't let go. Like a bulldog biting on a bone, she just kept gnawing. She wouldn't accept the police report that stated her husband committed suicide. Instead she fought, and when every gumshoe in the Air Capital told her to take a hike, she kept searching, kept trying until she stumbled onto a private dick just as crazy and tenacious as she was, yours truly. That was the killer's big mistake. He didn't figure anyone would keep coming after him, but he was wrong.

I checked my watch. It was almost nine o'clock, and I had some calls to make. Tom kept a phone booth in the corner. I got a bunch of nickels from him and climbed into the booth and closed the door behind me.

I dialed the police station first and wasn't surprised when the desk sergeant told me McCormick was off duty. I told the sergeant who I was and why I was calling.

"Call him at home," I said. "Find him and tell him it's urgent."

I gave the sergeant instructions on where McCormick should meet me. I called Lucille Hamilton next.

"Lucille, this is Pete. Listen, Lucille, I know it's late, but this is important. You've got to do exactly what I say."

I gave her instructions, and she assured me she would follow them. I checked my notebook for another number. I found it and dialed Gordon Veatch at home. He wasn't happy to be disturbed at that hour, especially by me, but when I told him what was up he listened quietly and agreed to do what I told him. The last call I made was to Agnes. I caught her just as she was removing her makeup and getting ready for bed.

"Listen, doll, something's come up, and I need you to work tonight."

What a gal. Agnes listened without interrupting, said "ok" in all the right places, agreed with what I said, and hung up. They don't make many dames like Agnes. After I hung up the phone, I climbed out of the booth and returned to the bar.

When Tom picked up my glass to refill it, I shook my head.

"Better give me some coffee, Tom. I need a clear head."

He did what I asked and set the steaming cup in front of me. I took a swallow and lit a cigarette.

"You look like a man on a mission," Tom said as he handed me my change.

"More like a man who's found the key to a locked door," I said. "Now it's time to turn the lock and see what's on the other side."

I finished my coffee and left.

I don't recall a single minute of the drive from Tom's Inn to the Hamilton home. That's where I was headed, and if the people I called had heeded my instructions, that's where a lot of other people would be, too. I drove automatically, without thinking about the traffic, the roadster, or anything to do with the trip. My mind was on crime, and I was anxious to see how tonight's events would unfold.

When did I first realize who the killer was? Was it today, at the ballpark watching a team of amateur's turn a few double plays? Was it while I was sitting at the bar, nursing a few beers and mulling over the details that had led to this moment? Or had I always suspected?

Several cars were parked in front of the Hamilton home when I pulled up. I parked behind a long sedan I recognized as Veatch's car and went in.

Lucille met me at the door and took my hat. She took one look at my battered face and uttered two words.

"Oh, Pete."

"It's okay, Lucille," I said. "I'll explain later."

She didn't say anything else, but she smiled and squeezed my arm in an encouraging way. I followed her into the living room. The night had turned cool, and Lucille had built a welcoming fire in the fireplace.

Ireland was there, sitting on the divan and sipping a cup of coffee. I'd asked Lucille to call him and ask him to come over, and, of course, she had. If he was surprised to see the other people in the room, he didn't let on. He was chatting with Agnes who also drank coffee beside him on the divan. McCormick smoked a cigarette and stood in front of the fireplace. Veatch sat in a wing-backed chair next to the fireplace and puffed on a cigar. Lucille offered me the other wing-backed chair, but I declined and had her take that chair. I sat on a straight-backed chair I carried in from the dining room. Everyone was assembled. The Chelsea Brass Marine clock over the fireplace read nine forty-five. Veatch spoke first.

"What the hell is this about, Stone? Excuse me, ladies. Stone, why are you dragging everyone over hell's half acre at this time of night? This better be good."

McCormick wanted to say something, but he looked as though Veatch had spoken for him, so he merely nodded his concurrence. The rest of the party sat quietly and waited for me to speak. I stood up and pushed the straight-backed chair to the side.

"Ladies and gentlemen," I said. "One of us in this room is a murderer."

I waited for the gasps to subside and continued.

"One of the people in this room is a murderer," I repeated.

"I don't believe you," Veatch said. "I do not believe you."

McCormick nodded but stayed silent.

"I didn't expect you to believe me, Mr. Veatch. So instead of pointing a finger and making an accusation, I'll step everyone through the events of the crime. Or should I say crimes, since we are talking about three murders after all?"

No one spoke.

"The first murder was that of Sidney Hamilton, of course, although that was ruled a suicide. Shortly after he was murdered, the Hamilton's neighbor, Alice Bennett was killed in her own garden. There's no question she was brutally murdered. Finally, a German visiting our city, Jonas Meier, was killed in his hotel room downtown, although, that killing, too, has been ruled a suicide."

I nodded to McCormick.

"Contrary to police investigation, Mac, all three of these deaths were murders."

"You've got the floor, Stone," Mac said. "This better be good."

I cleared my throat and continued.

"When investigating a murder, when considering a suspect, it's common to look for three simple elements. The first element is motive. Why did the suspect want to commit his crime, what need did the murder fulfill? The second element that must be present is the means. Did the suspect possess the ability to commit murder? Could he do it? The third and final element is opportunity. A suspect may possess the means and the motive, but without the opportunity, the crime is never committed. Once you determine who fits the profile, who possesses all three of these elements, identifying the murderer from among your suspects becomes quite easy. Unfortunately, identifying and proving all three of these elements is sometimes difficult to do."

McCormick stepped away from the fireplace and took the chair I had vacated. He lit another cigarette.

"Okay, Stone," he said. "I'm sure all of these good people are fascinated with your analysis and insight in detecting a murder. Make your point."

"In due time, Mac," I said. "As I say, making an accusation means nothing unless the elements I discussed are determined. Identifying the means to a murder is relatively easy, especially in a case like that involving Alice Bennett who was bludgeoned to death. Identifying the means in suspected suicides is a bit trickier, but that will be clear in a moment. The same goes for opportunity. It's relatively easy to determine how the murderer found the chance to kill his victim. No, the difficult element is motive. It's always motive that's so difficult to determine. In the final analysis, a sane person is left asking, why? Why was this person killed? Answering that question of 'why' takes more thought, more time, and it wasn't until earlier today that I finally got the answer. When that answer came to me, the other elements fell into place, leaving only one person as the suspect, the murderer, and that person is here this evening."

I paused to light a cigarette, not for dramatic effect, but because I wanted to gauge the reactions of those in the room. Lucille had her hand to her throat, knowing she was about to learn who killed her husband and neighbor. McCormick and Veatch both leaned forward, keenly interested in my next words. Agnes sat calmly and waited as if we were discussing nothing more interesting than politics. Ireland was the only one who fidgeted. He was the only one who needed to fidget.

"The murderer, ladies and gentlemen, is James Ireland."

Lucille was aghast. Ireland became indignant. Veatch appeared to be apoplectic. Mac looked puzzled, and Agnes, God bless Agnes, remained calm and stoic. Perhaps her eyebrow went up a bit. Ireland stuttered and spoke.

"Stone, you have no right to make that kind of accusation. Sidney Hamilton was my best friend. He was like a brother to me. We grew up together for Christ's sake!"

"Yes, that's right," I said. "Everything you say is true. That's what makes these murders so dastardly. You were Sidney Hamilton's best friend, and you killed him."

"Now see here, Stone," Veatch said. "I'll not have you sit there and accuse one of my employees of such acts without proof. You'd better have something good or I'll add slander to the charges I've filed against you."

"Oh, Pete, surely you must be wrong," Lucille said. "I've known James for years, and he and Sidney loved each other. They were like brothers. I want to know who killed Sidney, Pete, I do, but please be careful with what you say. Please don't let anyone else get hurt."

Mac crushed out another cigarette.

"This better be good, Stone," he said.

I cleared my throat again, and Agnes appeared at my elbow with a glass of water. I smiled at her and took a long swallow. She sat back down, once again leaving me the only person in the room standing. I moved toward the fireplace and faced the group.

"As I said earlier, determining who had the means and the opportunity to commit these murders is relatively easy. The list is quite long. At one time the list included several people."

I nodded toward Veatch who was sitting at my elbow.

"You were on the list, Mr. Veatch," I said, "as well as Jonas Meier until he turned up dead."

I stared at James Ireland.

"And, of course, you were on the list, too, Ireland," I said.

He leaned forward. Veins bulged on his neck, but he didn't speak.

"It was only when I considered motive that the list narrowed to one individual. Any one of you, I suppose, might have had a reason to kill Sidney Hamilton. He was, after all, working on a top secret project for an advanced aircraft bomb sighting device. Isn't that correct?"

Veatch stood up and looked like he might explode.

"Where did you get that information?" he said. "That's top secret!"

"Easy, easy," I said. "Frankly, I don't give a damn about your secret project, and I doubt if anyone else in this room does either. The point is, Sidney Hamilton was your lead engineer on that project, and that might make him the target for a murder, either by someone inside your company or outside. Someone from Germany, perhaps. Several people might have had motive to kill Sidney Hamilton."

Lucille dabbed at her eyes with a handkerchief. This was difficult on her, but it had to be done.

"No, Hamilton's murder alone wasn't enough to narrow the list to one person. For that, I had to determine who wanted to kill Alice Bennett. Only one person had the motive to kill her. That person was James Ireland."

Now Ireland came to his feet.

"Now wait a minute! I read the papers, too. The police have said that the Bennett murder was unrelated to Sidney's death. Sidney killed himself, and a person unknown killed Mrs. Bennett."

I nodded and motioned for Ireland to sit back down. He did.

"I know what the police report states," I said, "and to outside eyes that's how it appears. But two deaths in such a short time, two people who lived right across the street from each other is too big a coincidence, Mr. Ireland. I don't like coincidences and neither do the police."

McCormick nodded agreement.

"It took me awhile to figure out why you wanted to kill an innocent soul like Alice Bennett," I said, "and then it came to me. You were here with Mrs. Hamilton that day I spoke to Alice Bennett. It was the day I met you. Alice Bennett told me that she saw Mr. Hamilton return home the morning he disappeared. You were in this room when I said that. Little did I know then that I was instrumental in that poor woman's murder."

"What are you talking about, Stone?" McCormick said. "This makes no sense."

"I mentioned what Mrs. Bennett had told me. She said that she was working in her garden that Tuesday morning when Mr. Hamilton disappeared. She said that he returned home sometime around mid-morning, went inside the house for ten minutes or so, and left again. Mr. Ireland was present when I asked Mrs. Hamilton if she knew why her husband might return home."

"So what?" Ireland said. "So I was here. So what?"

"You were the only one who knew that Sidney Hamilton did not return home that morning. You were the only one who knew that it was *you* who came to the Hamilton house that day. *You* came to the house, and you were seen by Mrs. Bennett. She thought you were Sidney, and why wouldn't she? You both were the same size, you both dressed alike, even your mannerisms were the same. It would be easy for anyone to mistake the two of you from a distance. That terrified you. What if Alice Bennett later realized her mistake? What if she identified you?

"What you didn't know, what you couldn't have known was that Mrs. Bennett wore glasses and needed them to see clearly. She didn't wear them in the garden, vanity I suppose. I noticed how she squinted when she looked across the street to the Hamilton home. But she kept glasses in her pocket. She took them out the day I met her to read my business card. You didn't know that. You only knew she had seen you. She had just assumed she saw Mr. Hamilton, but she really saw you, and you knew it. You knew it, and you were terrified you'd be discovered, so you killed her. You killed a gentle, innocent woman, Ireland, and I pushed you to do it."

Ireland buried his face in his hands. His shoulders slumped.

"Oh, James, James, how could you?" Lucille said. "How could you be so cruel to kill my Sidney, your best friend, the man who loved you like a brother? And Alice, too? How, James, how?"

Lucille began sobbing. Ireland refused to look up.

"It was the oldest and simplest motive in the world, Lucille," I said. "It was jealousy that drove him to it. James was jealous of Sidney, and why wouldn't he be? Sidney had everything, starting with you. You told me once that you had dated James, but it was Sidney you married. It was Sidney whose career was taking off at Stearman. It was Sidney who was picked to design the plans for the bomb sighting device, a device that would no doubt make Stearman Aircraft an even more valuable property for a Boeing acquisition. Sidney had everything. Ireland lived in Sidney's shadow. He was Sancho Panza to the great Don Quixote. He was a mere squire to the man on a quest. He finally snapped."

I turned to Ireland.

"Isn't that about it, Ireland?" I said.

Ireland kept his face buried in his hands, but he nodded 'yes.'

The sounds of exhales filled the room along with muffled sobs. The fire in the fireplace crackled. McCormick stood up.

"Let's go, Ireland," he said.

Later, looking back, we would all wonder how we could have been so unprepared for the events that took place in the next minute. We were, after all, dealing with a murderer, a shell of the man he once was, yes, but a murderer nevertheless. How then, did Ireland manage to draw a gun on us? How did he manage to wrap his left arm around Agnes at the same time and pin her to his chest as a shield, all in one swift moment while the rest of us stood or sat and gaped in horror?

"Don't move," Ireland said. "This isn't over yet. I'm not going to hang. Now back off."

Agnes, bless her heart, looked terrified, but she held up like a trooper. I didn't know what was going to happen next, but I knew

James Ireland was not leaving with Agnes, not as long as I had a breath in my body.

"Give it up, Ireland," I said. "You've ruined enough lives. Give it up."

"Hah! You'd like that wouldn't you, Stone? Big, hotshot private eye. Well, I'm not licked yet. The Germans still want those plans, and they're willing to pay big for them! I intend to cash in, and when I do, I'll have all I need to live like a king far, far from here."

"Is that right?" I asked. "The Germans will pay big? Then why did you kill Meier?"

"He was a cheapskate," Ireland said, "a bum, but he isn't the only one. There'll be another one soon, another one willing to pay what those plans are worth."

I didn't know what else to do, so I started laughing, really big, loud guffaws.

"You don't even know where those plans are, Ireland. If you did, you would have cashed them in and left by now. You're licked, Ireland. You lose. You're a loser. You'll always be a loser."

My distraction worked. Ireland became so enraged he threw Agnes aside and pointed his gun at me and fired just as I dropped to my left and pulled my gun. I heard a bullet whiz past my ear and explode into something on the mantel. I aimed my gun at Ireland's chest and fired, pouring hot lead into his torso. When the smoke cleared, I saw that McCormick had drawn and fired, too. Altogether, six shots had found their mark. Ireland lay dead.

I removed my coat and put it over the body. The ladies retreated to the kitchen, and McCormick used the phone to call for the coroner. Veatch lit a cigar and shook his head. When McCormick returned, he began with the questions. I gave him as many answers as I had.

Ireland had come to the Hamilton home that Tuesday morning to get the bottle of barbiturates he knew Hamilton sometimes took to help him sleep. Ireland had wanted Hamilton's murder to look like a suicide, so he gave the barbiturates to him probably in his coffee or other drink. They made him drowsy but didn't kill him, so Ireland got him into the car and drove him to the river where he drowned him.

We'd already covered the murder of Alice Bennett, but that left Jonas Meier. Why did he have to die? Probably, as Ireland had said, because Meier hadn't come through with enough money. But Ireland wouldn't have killed Meier unless he knew he'd have another German agent to work with. I showed McCormick Meier's appointment book and ignored his outrage at my withholding of evidence. I showed him the notation "HLNASt" dated May 6th.

"I guess a German visitor named H. L. Nast is expected tomorrow," I said.

McCormick and Veatch both nodded.

"There is one other thing," Veatch said. "What with all this killing, I hate to bring this up, but our plans are still missing for what is, or at least used to be, a top secret project. Now that Ireland is dead, we may never find those plans. I refuse to believe Hamilton sold us out to the Germans. He must have hidden them somewhere, but where?"

I glanced at the Chelsea Brass Marine clock on the mantel. The bullet Ireland had intended for me caught the clock and destroyed it. The timepiece was ruined, but the mahogany base was intact. I read the inscription: "Time is the justice that examines all offenders." Something came to me, and I recalled my recent conversation with my son, Dan, about the strides in microfilm development. Could Sidney have been aware of this? Of course, he could have. An engineer of his caliber would have stayed abreast of anything new and revolutionary.

I took the clock off the mantel and noted that the plaque bearing the inscription was secured to the base by tiny screws. I took out my pocket knife and turned the screws.

"What are you doing, Stone?" McCormick said.

"Playing a hunch, Mac. Hold on."

I removed the plaque and uncovered a small compartment. Something was inside. I turned the clock over and a small roll of film fell out.

"I believe this is what you're looking for, Mr. Veatch," I said.

Veatch tossed his cigar into the fire and took the film. He unrolled several inches and held it up to the light.

"Well, I'll be a son-of-a-bitch," he said. "Mr. Stone, you amaze me. You've just performed a great service for your country."

He took my hand and shook it while Mac rolled his eyes. The coroner arrived and removed the body. Mac and Veatch left, and Agnes stood at the door. She put on her hat and coat, and I gave her a hug.

"See you tomorrow, Pete," she said.

"Okay, doll. Let's give ourselves a treat. How about nine o'clock?" I said.

"How about nine-thirty?" Agnes said.

"Let's make it ten."

Agnes looked at Lucille and then at me, and she smiled.

"It looks like you got your man," she said and winked.

Was she talking to me or Lucille? I watched her from the door until she got in her car and drove away. Then I closed the door and took Lucille in my arms and held her close for several long minutes.

Next in the Pete Stone Series

Shadow of Death

by Michael D. Graves

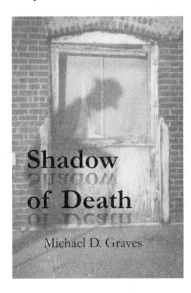

Copyright © 2017 Michael D. Graves
meadowlark-books.com
ISBN: 978-0-9966801-6-5
Library of Congress Control Number: 2017915462

Saturday, June 5

The first time I met the cop we had words. You might've called it an altercation. Maybe even a fight. It was night, late at night, going into the wee hours of the morning, and I'd been drinking, again. I'd been drinking a lot lately. The cop braced me on the sidewalk down the street from Tom's Inn, planting a fleshy paw on my chest with a stiff arm. He flashed a grin that bore not a trace of good humor. He leaned in and sniffed my breath and snapped his head back.

"Ugh, man. You smell like a drunken bum. You're stink-o, you are. Who are you, buddy? What's your name?"

I fumbled through my pockets and pulled out a card.

"Pete Stone, Private Investigations," he said. "So, you're a gumshoe. Well, you're drunk, gumshoe. I hope you don't think you're going to drive your fancy automobile over my city streets in your condition. Cause if you do, you've got another think coming."

I stood under a yellow streetlight. My Jones Six Roadster, top down, was parked at the curb three steps away. My keys dangled from my fingertips. I glanced at my car. I glanced at my keys. I looked at the cop.

"Wise deduction, Sherlock," I said. I may have slurred. "How'd you figure that?"

Tom and I had spent the better part of the evening perched on barstools, swapping stories and lies, and lowering the level of a bottle of rye whiskey. We'd discussed our lives, what we'd done, what we hadn't done, what we wished we hadn't done. We'd bounced around the country's problems and agreed the solution to halting the current Depression was to boot out the politicians and replace them each year with whichever team won the World Series. We'd proclaimed that the humblest barbeque in Jerkwater, Kansas tasted better than the finest steak in Delmonico's Restaurant, never mind that neither of us had ever eaten a steak at Delmonico's or any other fine restaurant in New York City. And we'd pondered why the women we loved always broke our hearts and we kept coming back for more. It was the pondering over one woman in particular that had led me to the bottle, the barstool, and to bending the ear of my longtime pal and confidant, Tom, owner of the inn bearing his name.

Now it was late, the whiskey was gone, the inn was closed, and I was on the sidewalk, weaving on wobbly pins in front of a beat cop. I was filled to the gills with wisdom, wit, and bullet-proof courage. The cop was unimpressed.

"Okay, wise guy. Give me the keys. You're not driving anywhere."

That seemed an unreasonable request. Then again, I was in no condition to be reasonable. I puffed out my chest like an idiot and said something stupid that besmirched the cop's parentage. His eyes grew wide, and a vein bulged on his neck. His hand went for his nightstick. My arms went up, and I heard, or felt, an explosion. For an instant, it was all rockets and a light show blazing in my skull, then the lights dimmed and faded into darkness. Later, I would swear that's all I could remember. After that, however, I would be consumed with doubt.

The next time I saw the cop he lay in the morgue, stretched out on a slab. My hands were cuffed, my head throbbed, and my vision was blurry, but I could make out the third eye in the cop's forehead, the one the bullet had put there. My aching ribs made each breath an exercise in pain, and hammers clanged in my skull, but I could process a thought. I had heard the voice, I had listened to the charges, and I knew where I stood. A cop lay dead, murdered. I was found lying next to him, out cold but breathing. My .38 Smith & Wesson, with a spent cartridge, lay on the sidewalk next to me. How and why my gun came to be there was a mystery to me. I couldn't explain it. I had no memory of pulling the trigger. No one else was around, but someone had seen or heard something. Someone had made the call. I was arrested, cuffed, and tossed into jail. Maybe the arresting officers had jumped to conclusions. Maybe they hadn't. I was in no condition to argue. I was in deep trouble, and I knew it. I was booked on a murder charge. I was booked as the sole suspect in the murder of one of Wichita's finest. I was accused of killing a cop.

Sunday, June 6

A ll of that took place on Saturday night, more likely Sunday morning. I was too sore to know or care. By the time the cops tossed me into my cell, I'd been beaten and broken, and the last thing on my mind was the day or the time. I lay atop a urine-stained mattress, too sore to sleep and too exhausted not to. Every so often I'd roll out of bed and crawl the mile or so to the toilet in the corner of the cell to either vomit or dry heave, further adventures in pain and discomfort.

Eventually, I sobered. I was still boozed up, but I was no longer drunk. That wasn't necessarily a good thing. The more I sobered, the worse the pain felt. Room service at the crowbar hotel included being beaten until I'd blacked out, more than once. The body inside my tattered suit felt like a single raw wound. The blood caked on the front of my shirt reminded me that my lip had been split open and my nose battered. My fingers probed and inspected the cuts. My bruised eyes were swollen nearly shut. My ribs ached with every breath.

I lay on the cot, and recollections came to me. I'd been standing in a circle of uniformed cops and passed back and forth, a human punching bag. One guy had kidney-punched me and passed me on to another who took a shot at my face before another cop kicked me in the ribs and kneed me in the stomach.

Around and around I went. The cops were kids at a birthday party, and I was the piñata. A cop killer brought out the best in the boys in blue.

I closed my eyes and tried to think of something more pleasant, less painful. I did what I often do when I have long moments alone and time to kill. I thought about baseball. My thoughts went back to a year ago, in early May, when I was working on a case in Missouri. I'd stopped in a diner, and a radio was broadcasting a baseball game on KMOX out of St. Louis. France Laux was calling the game. A young rookie for the New York Yankees named Joe DiMaggio was playing his first big league game against the St. Louis Browns. The rookie showed a lot of promise, going three for six that day, including a triple. Laux described the scene. Joe DiMaggio cocked his bat and crouched in his wide stance, waiting for Jack Knott to deliver the pitch. The pitch came in low and fast, and DiMaggio swung the bat, and there was a crack as the hard ash connected with horsehide.

A gasp brought me out of my reverie. A woman stood outside my cell and watched me through the bars. She covered the lower half of her face with the back of one hand. She carried something in her other hand, a tray it seemed, but my eyesight was too blurred to tell for sure. For a moment, the woman stood frozen in place, unsure what to do next. Neither of us spoke.

She lowered her hand from her mouth and grasped the object with both hands. My eyes focused, and I could make out a tray. She lifted something from it. With one hand, she slid the tray through a slot in the bars, resting it on a narrow shelf mounted inside the cell. With the other hand, she reached through the bars and placed a cup on the tray. Then she lowered her eyes and turned and walked off. I listened to the tapping of her heels fade away.

(excerpt from Shadow of Death, book II in the Pete Stone Series)

daveleikerphotography.com

About the Author

About the Author

Michael D. Graves teaches Intensive English and TESOL courses at Emporia State University. His writing has appeared in *Cheap Detective Stories*, *Thorny Locust*, *Flint Hills Review*, and elsewhere. He is an author of *Green Bike, a group novel*, along with Kevin Rabas and Tracy Million Simmons. When life conjures its riddles, he turns to back roads and baseball for answers.

If you enjoyed this book,

please write a review!

Acknowledgments
ACKNOWLEDGMENTS

Writing a book isn't a solo endeavor, and I appreciate those who helped me along the way. I'd like to thank those who read early drafts: Jennifer Brice, Theresa Danby, Daryl Graves, Heather Graves, Monica Graves, Rick Graves, Sharon Graves, Anita Hind, Sherry Hind, Bill Lang, and Connie Lang. Thank you for your comments and encouragement.

Thanks to the good people at The Wichita-Sedgwick County Historical Museum and The Kansas Aviation Museum who are keeping Wichita's past alive. Thank you to the kind folks at The Wichita Public Library and The Kansas Historical Society for providing a wealth of historical information and for their patience and assistance as I pored over microfilmed *Wichita Eagle* newspapers.

Thank you, Kevin Rabas, friend and writer, for your advice. I appreciate your notes of encouragement and look forward to more Chinese food together.

Thank you, Dave Leiker, for wandering the alleys and shooting the perfect shadows. You are an artist, and your cover photos are terrific.

Thank you, Tracy Million Simmons, for reading, editing, and advising. Each of your suggestions improved the book. I'm also grateful to you and to Meadowlark Books for your creative design work and for bringing this novel to life.

And finally, thank you to my wife, Monica, for knowing when to be there and when to give me space. When I struggle with the lyrics, you bring the music.

Read

A Meadowlark Book

Nothing feels better than home

While we at Meadowlark Books love to travel, we also cherish our home time. We are nourished by our open prairies, our enormous skies, community, family, and friends. We are rooted in this land, and that is why Meadowlark Books publishes regional authors.

When you open one of our fiction books, you'll read delicious stories that are set in the Heartland. Settle in with a volume of poetry, and you'll remember just how much you love this place too—the landscape, its skies, the people.

Meadowlark Books publishes memoir, poetry, short stories, and novels. Read stories that began in the Heartland, that were written here. Add to your Meadowlark Book collection today.

Specializing in Books by Authors from the Heartland Since 2014

Made in the USA
Monee, IL
04 June 2023

35012012R00121